# A LOVE TO CHERISH

LINDA FORD

# CHAPTER 1

GLORY, MONTANA, SPRING 1884

Reese Cartwright rode his black horse, Thunder, down the dusty main street of the small town of Glory, Montana. He and the man who had joined him three days ago drew abreast of White's Store. Two young ladies stepped to the wooden sidewalk, not more than ten feet away. Reese glanced at them. His glance turned into a surprised gape as the pair walked away.

"That looks like Constance Hayworth." He blurted the words out without forethought. Same pale blonde hair—the color of sunshine. The same sky-blue eyes. So bright they were visible from where he sat on his horse. Of course, there were dozens of blue-eyed blondes. It was unlikely this was the same girl.

"The missin' daughter of that rich man? I remember

hearin' 'bout it. Wasn't there a generous reward offered for information about her?"

The greed in the man's voice was unmistakable. Reese knew little about the cowboy at his side. Name: Smitty. Reason to be riding this way: to find a job in Montana Territory. Reese hadn't given the lack of information much thought. Over the past few years, he'd ridden days and weeks with all sorts of men and learned nothing about them save their name and how well they handled cows.

He wished he hadn't said anything about the girl. After all, it was simply a gut reaction. "That was four years ago. I'm sure Miss Hayworth has been reunited with her family by now. This gal simply bears a resemblance to what I remember of the girl. But then, I only glimpsed her a time or two." She was from a rich family. Reese was not. In fact, as soon as he was old enough, he started working at the Hayworth Foundry as had his Pa and his stepfather.

"You thinking youse can keep all the reward money to yerself?"

"Not at all." If Reese hadn't blurted out the name, Smitty would have no idea how much she looked like the girl he remembered seeing back in Chicago. "But I don't have time to chase after an old reward likely no longer offered. I've got a ranch to buy and run. Been aiming for exactly that for several years."

"Look at it anyway ya like."

Smitty reined in. "Guess this is where we part ways. I'm heading north to that ranch I heard about. Been nice to ride with ya awhile." He sketched a goodbye and trotted down the street.

Reese watched until all that remained of the departing man was a swirl of dust in the distance. Somehow, he didn't think that was the last he'd see of him. Nor that he would ride off without looking into the reward money that had once been offered. Four years ago. No doubt the need was long ago over.

But Smitty could upset the girl's life by poking about in her business.

Was it even remotely possible the Hayworth girl was still missing? He couldn't imagine that Mr. Hayworth hadn't turned over every stone across the entire country until he found his daughter.

And yet, the young lady he'd seen bore an uncanny resemblance to the girl as he remembered her. He'd never forget how her eyes slanted upward giving the impression she wore a permanent smile. The girl outside the store had the same slanting eyes, but surely it was only coincidence. Why would she be here? Not knowing, carrying suspicion in his thoughts, left him ill at ease.

Maybe he'd hang around a few days and ask a few questions. He wasn't interested in the reward money nor did he care if Mr. Hayworth had succeeded in his search.

His only concern was in uncovering the truth.

Truth, he'd learned, was a rare commodity. But without it, life carried a sour taste. His association with Betty Collins had taught him that lesson well and good. He didn't mean to repeat it.

If there was something strange afoot, he meant to find out and put things right. For the sake of everyone involved. Yes, he could simply walk away, and he was more than half tempted to. He'd never forgotten Mr. Hayworth's high-handed, harsh ways of questioning the workers at the foundry, ready to believe one of them had been involved in his daughter's disappearance.

He wasn't doing this for Mr. Hayworth but for himself. After Betty, he'd vowed to challenge any hint of untruth.

He turned and rode back to the store, tied Thunder to the hitching post, and went inside. "Howdy," he said to the man behind the counter. A man in his thirties, Reese guessed, with brown hair, brown eyes, and a brown handlebar moustache. His brown shirt made his color scheme complete.

"Howdy, yourself. Don't believe I've seen you around before."

"Nope. Just rode in."

"What brings you to Glory?"

"I heard of a little ranch for sale west of here." He'd already been in touch with Abe Shaw, had made an offer, and had it accepted.

"The Shaw place? I heard he was selling. Too much sorrow for him there."

Reese knew a bit of why Abe Shaw was selling out but thought he might learn more from the storekeeper. And he didn't just mean about the ranch. "I heard he'd suffered some losses."

"That's a fact. His wife and two young ones died last winter. Pneumonia, they say. Now what can I do for you, mister?"

"Reese Cartwright." He held his hand toward the man.

"Norm White." They shook and then Norm waved his hand about the store. "I carry most everything you'll need to run a ranch or a house. Say, you married?"

Good. A perfect opening into the questions Reese

had. "Nope. Haven't had time." No need to tell the man he'd once considered it, but Betty had turned out to be only proving to her friends she could make Reese fall in love with her. And he had. He'd given her his heart, open and free. She'd had no intention of returning the sentiment. When she laughed and told him the truth, he'd been devastated. Humiliated and hurt beyond imagination. Never again, he vowed.

He leaned closer to Mr. White and managed to look shy and ready to begin courting. "Any young ladies around here who might be interested?"

The storekeeper chuckled. "Indeed there is. Preacher Kinsley has three unmarried daughters. In fact, two of the girls left here moments ago."

Reese straightened. "I believe I saw them. One was blonde if I recall. The other had black hair. Quite a contrast for sisters."

"Well, they're adopted, so they don't have to look alike."

Adopted? That changed things to a degree, but just because the girl was in the preacher's family didn't give him any assurance that there was no possibility of an underhanded scheme. Betty had been a church-going, well-respected person. But one with no moral fortitude. "The blonde one. Was she adopted as a baby, do you know?"

"Can't say as I do. You interested in her?"

"I only glimpsed her, but I saw enough to know she's downright pretty."

"That's Miss Victoria, and pretty she certainly is."

Could Victoria and Constance be the same person? Like he'd said to Smitty, the resemblance was surely coincidental. Still, he had to make sure. He wouldn't have any peace of mind until he was certain one way or the other.

"The Kinsleys been in this area long? Where did they come from, do you know?" He pointed out some items he wanted as he talked, and Mr. White began stacking goods on the counter.

"They came a few months ago." The man leaned back on his heels and stroked his moustache. "Say, aren't you asking a lot of questions about them? There something special you want to know?"

Reese considered asking directly when Miss Victoria had joined the family, but the man was growing suspicious already, and if the Kinsleys had recently moved into the area, how much would the man know? "Just curious. Guess maybe I'd like to get to know that pretty gal a bit better."

Mr. White nodded, apparently satisfied that Reese's questions were those of a young man interested in a certain young woman. "The best advice I can give you is to show up at church tomorrow. Mrs. Kinsley asks cowboys to join them for dinner after the service."

"Thanks for telling me." He paid for the goods and left the store. He had hoped to ride out to the ranch and talk to Abe about arranging its purchase, but it could wait until after he'd been to church.

The next morning, Reese donned the new shirt and trousers he'd purchased. He'd gotten his hair cut at the barbershop the day before. He examined his likeness in the tiny mirror he carried with him.

"Not bad," he told his reflection, then sighed. "About as good as it gets."

He left his horse grazing by the river and made his way toward the church. It was early, and he stood where he could watch those coming to the service. A man in a black suit crossed from the house next to the church. "Likely Preacher Kinsley," he murmured. A moment later, a young lady followed. She wore a bonnet, so he couldn't see for sure the color of her hair, but she was taller than he thought Miss Victoria to be. Then she turned slightly. It was the dark-haired one from yesterday. The girl entered the church and Reese soon heard the sound of a piano.

People began to arrive at the front of the church. A buggy with an older couple. A wagon with several children who scrambled out the back as soon as it stopped. Half a dozen cowboys on horseback. Still he waited, wanting to see more of the family.

Two women stepped from the house. He recognized the blonde girl from yesterday and strained to see her better. He hadn't seen Miss Hayworth in more than four years—shortly before her disappearance, and only as she rode past in a buggy accompanied by her father. At the time, he'd thought her the most beautiful girl he'd ever seen. The way she smiled made him think she had a sweet nature. When she'd smiled at him, he'd been mesmerized by her eyes—so blue, so kind looking. He'd stared at her until his stepfather had cuffed him on the side of the head and told him to mind his manners.

He'd seen her close by on only one other occasion. He'd walked by her fine house, angry at his stepfather for some reason and needing to get as far away from him as possible. He hadn't realized he was passing the Hayworth house until he saw Miss Constance bent over a rose bush. Even knowing he would be soundly reprimanded —perhaps even subjected to a beating if one of the servants saw him staring at the daughter of the important Mr. Hayworth—he had stopped to admire the picture she made.

This woman had the same profile he remembered. The same upright carriage. The same generous smile as she spoke to the older lady at her side whom Reese took to be the mother.

Two more women left the house. Both were rather colorless in comparison to the one named Victoria. Two young children held hands and followed.

As they crossed the yard, another wagon stopped. A redheaded woman jumped down and ran to the group. "Ma," she cried, and hugged the older woman.

A tall, lean man followed the redhead. Reese studied him. He'd seen men like him before. Loners. Tough as an ax handle. And yet the man smiled at the women, his widest smile for the redhead.

Reese made his way across the yard, timing his steps so he arrived at the entrance to the church at the same time as those he'd been watching. He hoped he might overhear something that would explain this situation, but their talk seemed to be about family things—meals, gardens—nothing that helped him understand. Nothing to assure him this young woman with the striking resemblance to Miss Hayworth could not possibly be her.

He entered the church a few steps behind the redhead and the man he assumed was her husband and slipped into a pew that allowed him to watch the family. The preacher took his place behind the pulpit and the dark-haired daughter played the piano as they sang hymns. Hymns that Reese hadn't heard in a long time. He had quit church after Betty although the main reason he didn't go was there weren't churches on a cattle drive or near most of the ranches where he'd worked. For a time, he'd welcomed the excuse for not attending services. However, he no longer blamed God for how Betty had treated him.

The song service ended, and Reese listened keenly to the sermon, trying to detect any hint of hypocrisy. Instead, he heard sincerity and love.

Either this man was an excellent charlatan, or he didn't know the identity of the girl in the midst of his family. Or she had no connection to Miss Hayworth. He was more and more inclined to believe the latter.

But Reese couldn't let it go until he was certain. He owed it to the missing girl. Partly because of how he'd carried the pleasure of her smile in his heart for a long time and partly because he knew Smitty wouldn't let go of the promise of the reward money.

But mostly because he believed so strongly in knowing the truth, speaking the truth, and living truth to the best of his ability.

\* \* \*

VICTORIA HURRIED home after the service and helped put out the meal. As was Ma's custom, several cowboys had been invited to join them for dinner. Eve and Josie scurried about in the kitchen. Stella Norwood, the widow who had come to them a month ago, too ill and weak to walk to the church, sank wearily into a chair. Her children, Blossom and Donny, stayed at her knees, impatiently waiting for the meal.

Flora entered with Kade on her heels. Victoria stopped to study them.

"What?" Flora asked, brushing her hands over her dress as if to remove dust.

Victoria chuckled. "I still have a hard time picturing you as a married woman." She laughed when Flora colored up.

Flora tossed her heavy braids to her back. "I have to admit it's taking me some time to get used to the idea."

Kade pressed a kiss to Flora's forehead. "I hope that's a good thing."

Flora gave Kade a look of such adoration that Victoria glanced away, feeling she intruded into a private moment.

Pa led three cowboys into the kitchen and Ma hustled everyone to their seats. As usual, she placed one of the girls next to each cowboy. The girls had often shared a laugh at Ma's matchmaking.

"I'm only using whatever means I have at my disposal to get these young men to attend church," Ma protested.

Victoria didn't mind getting them to church, but she wasn't interested in matchmaking. She didn't know who she was, which made it impossible to think of romance and love. Her biggest fear was falling in love then regaining her memory and forgetting the man she loved. The doctor had assured her that after four years, it was possible, but highly unlikely, that she would ever remember who she was, but it was small consolation. She had no past. Who was she, besides one of the Kinsley girls?

Pa asked the blessing, and the food was passed from hand to hand. When everyone had been served, Pa, as was his habit, asked the cowboys to tell a little bit about themselves. Two of the cowboys had been there before. Rather bland young men named Arnie and Teller. Victoria thought the most interesting thing about the pair was the latter's name. He'd been asked about it but simply said it was his given name.

Everyone turned to the third man.

"My name is Reese Cartwright." He'd already been introduced but seemed to think he needed to begin with his name.

Victoria widened her eyes so as to not blink at the deep rumbling voice of the man. He was certainly handsome with his black hair and black eyes and a smile that promised happiness and sunshine.

*Really, Victoria,* she scolded herself.

Pa asked for more details about the man.

"I'm originally from Chicago." His gaze met Victoria's. Something flickered through his dark eyes. Was it more than casual interest? Was it recognition?

She ducked her head, her heart hammering against her ribs. Did he know who she was? Why did she always wonder the same thing when any stranger looked at her? It was an unsettling feeling.

He continued. "I left about four years ago to join a cattle drive. Been doing that ever since but now I'm planning to buy the Shaw ranch."

"I heard he was moving out," Pa said. "Such a tragedy losing his wife and children." Then Pa leaned closer to Reese. "You married?"

"No sir."

"Any plans to do so?"

"Not in the near future."

Pa sat back and studied the man. Victoria thought Pa was silently measuring him for a wedding suit and ducked her head to hide a grin.

But she couldn't resist sharing the humor of the situation and looked at Reese. "Pa's considering you as a prospective son-in-law."

"Victoria Kinsley." Ma was shocked at Victoria's boldness, but Victoria barely heard her as she held the dark gaze of the man across the table.

Pa chuckled. "She might be more right than I care to admit."

"Did you have a daughter picked out for me?" Reese asked.

"There's three of them right here. All good girls who will make excellent wives."

"Not me." Victoria shook her head.

Both Eve and Josie protested. "Pa, we'll be choosing our own man, thanks."

Two cowboys looked eagerly from one girl to the next, but Victoria continued to hold Reese's gaze.

"In the service of truth, I have to say I'm not really interested in a wife at the moment." Something flickered through the man's eyes, and Victoria wondered what lay behind his assertion.

He shifted his gaze to Pa, leaving Victoria feeling dizzy and disorientated. Although she had often felt that way when she tried to remember who she was, it had not happened since they moved to Glory, Montana Territory, and she did not thank the cowboy across the table for causing it again.

He gave a thin smile. "I'll be too busy ranching to have time for a wife."

Ma suggested they should serve dessert and Victoria jumped up so fast, Ma laughed.

"It's not that urgent."

Eve and Josie gave Victoria quizzical looks as they helped serve the cake.

As she returned to her place at the table, Victoria slowed her breathing and forced her thoughts to something that made sense. "Pa, I'm glad you reminded everyone at church about the talent show and box social on Friday." She glanced about the table, carefully looking at each person without looking directly at the newcomer. "If it goes well, we should have enough money to build a schoolhouse."

Josie paused from eating her cake to address those at the table. "What you all need to understand is that this is Victoria's dream. She wants to see the children of the community properly educated. So, she began the schoolhouse fund. So, she's hoping...we're all hoping, you come to the event on Friday. Be prepared to spend a dollar or two. Who knows?" Her brown eyes sparkled, and she grinned at those around the table. "You might buy the box lunch of one of us."

Young Arnie leaned forward. "How will we know which box to bid on?"

"Just look for the prettiest boxes."

Victoria had decided to allow herself no more study of Reese, but she couldn't stop herself from looking his way to see if he seemed interested in the upcoming event.

His dark eyes watched her intently.

She lowered her gaze to the table. Was he more interested in her than he should be? Given that he wasn't looking for a mate, why did he study her so intently? A flame of anger burned her insides. She'd thought moving to Montana Territory had freed her of this fear of encountering someone who knew who she was. It was unsettling and she didn't like it one bit.

"I'll plan to be there," he said.

Why should she think he meant the words for her?

Unless he knew who she was.

Fear and hope tangled through her insides making it difficult for her to draw in a satisfying breath and even more difficult to follow the conversation around the table.

"Why don't you young folk go enjoy the sunshine? Flora and I will clean up the kitchen."

Three cowboys were instantly on their feet, extending thanks and looking eager to do Ma's bidding.

"But Ma—"

Ma cut off Eve's protests and made a shooing motion.

Josie caught her arm. "Come on. It's a beautiful day." She reached toward Victoria, but Victoria backed away and considered her options.

Arnie and Teller were at the door, hats in hand. Reese hesitated as if waiting for Victoria to indicate what she planned to do. She should be flattered that it seemed to matter to him if she joined the group, but her nerves tingled that he seemed interested in her.

Should she stay behind or face her fears?

Knowing that running away did not solve anything, she made up her mind and followed the others out. She hurried to join Eve, hoping to cling to her side, but Teller had fallen in step with her. Arnie and Josie walked side by side leaving Victoria no choice but to either appear rude or walk at Reese's side. She chose the latter.

"The sun is exceptionally bright today," she said. They walked west. The sun glistened off the mountains. She filled her lungs. "The mountains always make me feel safe." Now why had she said such a silly thing?

"'I will lift up mine eyes unto the hills, from whence cometh my help. My help cometh from the Lord, which made heaven and earth.'"

"You're quoting the One Hundredth and Twenty-first Psalm." In her mind, she quoted the last verse of the passage. A verse that she turned to often for comfort. *The Lord shall preserve thy going out and thy coming in from this time forth, and even forever more.*

He chuckled, a deep satisfying sound that matched his talking voice. "You needn't sound so surprised. I have hidden many verses in my heart."

"That you might not sin against Him?" she teased, quoting the rest of the verse.

"That, of course. But also, because they comfort me and guide me. Besides, one can't always have a Bible with them."

"I find great comfort and encouragement in the Scriptures." Surely this was a safe topic of discussion. The others had gotten far enough ahead that Victoria and Reese carried on their own conversation.

"Me too. Though it wasn't always so."

"Why is that?"

He shrugged. "I had to learn difficult lessons in order to realize that God is faithful."

Surprised at how sincere he sounded, so unlike most

of the cowboys she'd met, Victoria slowed her steps to study him. "Me too." Goodness, she did not want him asking any personal questions, so she quickly added, "What kind of lessons?"

"Looking back, they don't seem as important as they did at the time. They were just a part of life and growing up." He turned his gaze to the mountains, allowing her to study him without appearing to stare.

His gaze still on the distance, he continued. "My pa died when I was fifteen. I took care of Ma for a time but then she remarried. Suffice it to say, my stepfather didn't care to share his home with a grown son, so I left and joined a Texas cattle drive. Turns out it was the best thing that ever happened to me." He brought his gaze to her. "What about you? What lessons did you have to learn?"

She couldn't tell him that she was a woman with amnesia who didn't know who she was. But she felt she had to tell him something after he'd shared so honestly. "That God is with me wherever I go, and I can trust Him."

"It's a great lesson, but I'm curious as to what circumstances led you to that."

"It wasn't just one thing, but a long journey. For instance, moving here. I didn't know what the future held." Any more than she knew what her past looked like. "I suppose you could say that I've had to learn to walk day by day with God."

He watched her, his eyes full of something she couldn't identify. Didn't want to. But if she had to, she would say he found her answer less than satisfactory.

But what more could she offer? It was no secret that

she had amnesia, but neither did she feel she had to tell everyone. It wasn't just a desire to avoid speculation and questions about what it was like not to remember.

No, it was mostly because she constantly feared someone would recognize her.

Or that no one ever would.

She turned to the west. She quoted another verse that steadied her. "'As the mountains are round about Jerusalem, so the Lord is round about his people from henceforth even for ever.'" She picked up the pace to bring them closer to the others.

Reese spoke quietly. "You have not always lived here, and yet you quote verses about God's care being like the mountains."

She nodded. "Seeing the mountains here in Montana Territory made me realize how strong and mighty God's care is."

"You have a loving, supportive family, and yet you talk like life is full of scary things. Why is that?"

"It's—I'm not—but—" How was she to answer this man's questions without saying more than she cared to?

What was worse—not knowing her past or fearing it?

## CHAPTER 2

Reese had tried and failed to get any information from Victoria. He needed more before he would be thoroughly convinced she wasn't the missing Hayworth girl. They caught up to the others and the six of them sat on the banks of Buck River. From his correspondence with Abe Shaw, Reese knew it was the same river that flowed through the ranch he meant to buy and he asked a few questions of the two cowboys. He learned it ran deep and wild in the late spring when the snow melted from the mountains and flowed all summer, providing good watering for cattle.

The others talked about the upcoming talent show.

"You gals doing something in the talent show?" Arnie asked.

"Yes, we are," Eve answered.

"What?" Teller asked.

Josie gave him a teasing smile. "I guess you'll have to come and see for yourself."

"All of you?" Reese asked, careful not to look at Victoria.

"You'll have to come and see," Josie repeated.

"I'll do that."

The other cowboys echoed him.

"That's good," Josie said.

"You be sure and invite all your friends," Victoria added. "We need lots of people to come out."

"You're certainly anxious to get the school built." Reese wondered if there was a reason it was so important to her. Other than the obvious one that the children needed to learn to read and write, though many of them would learn to do so with their parents' instruction.

"I love books and learning and want the children to experience the same joy."

Reese digested that information. "It sounds like you've had the privilege of a good education. Where did you get that?"

A stillness that was palpable met his question. He shifted to look at the girls to his right. Eve and Josie watched him. Victoria, at his elbow, twisted a blade of grass between her fingers.

"Did I say something wrong?" He wondered if anyone would tell him who this gal was and why she was here.

"She doesn't remember," Eve said.

Victoria sucked in air.

"How can you forget where you went to school?" It didn't make sense.

Victoria got to her feet. "Did you hear that? It sounded like a bear whoofing."

Reese thought she likely heard her own indrawn breath.

The other girls got up too. "We better get back."

Reese joined the others on the trek back to the manse. Victoria clung to a sister on either side, leaving the cowboys to follow in their wake. He obviously wasn't going to get any more information from Victoria this afternoon.

He'd be back Friday for the talent show and box social. And somehow, he'd discover the truth about her.

HE SPENT the night in town, camped out by the river. By morning he had come to a decision. He would ride out and speak to Abe then return to town. If possible, he'd find a job and hang around, learning more about the mysterious Miss Victoria. Only, he informed himself, because he cared about the truth.

As soon as it was light, he rode north, following directions to the Shaw ranch. With every passing mile, he grew more pleased with his decision to buy the ranch. The land was hilly with bunches of trees, lots of grass, and a number of watering holes besides the river that he followed. Ideal ranching country.

He recognized the place from Abe's description. A low house. A barn that would be more than adequate and several outbuildings.

A man stepped from the barn at Reese's approach. "Howdy, stranger. What brings you this way?"

"Abe? Abe Shaw? I'm Reese Cartwright." He swung from the saddle and the two shook hands. Three hours later, Reese rode back to Glory, satisfied with the business he had conducted. He would move to the ranch in two weeks, giving Abe time to wrap up his affairs. Reese had purchased the stock as well.

Finally, his dream was about to come true. A place of his own. Something solid he could count on. At one time he would have included in his dream someone to welcome him home after a day's work. But he had closed his heart to that part of his future. Betty, with her falseness, had taught him there were worse things than being alone… There was trusting someone who was false. Building your life on a lie.

Which brought his thoughts back to Victoria. Was she pretending one thing while being another? Even though it was none of his business, he intended to find out. In a quest for truth.

That day he found work at the livery barn. He warned the owner, Mickey, it would be temporary, but that was fine with the man. As Reese cleaned out the stalls, he tried to come up with a plan for spending more time with Victoria.

He guessed from her reaction Sunday afternoon that she might shy away from a direct question. That left him with few options.

The next day, his chores at the livery barn completed, he sauntered along Main Street and parked himself on the bench outside White's Store. It allowed him a good view of the activities of town. If he leaned forward, he caught sight of the corner of the church, but the manse stood behind it and out of view.

It was early afternoon and the Kinsley girls might be busy with something, but he was a patient man, and he waited.

A young lad Reese would guess to be around ten or

eleven sauntered by accompanied by a black and white dog. The boy slowed his steps and watched Reese from the corner of his eyes then jogged to the wide wooden steps and rested one foot on a step to lean on his knee.

"Ain't seen you before."

"Got here a day or two ago." They studied each other casually, as if not really interested. Amusement trickled Reese's insides at the boy's careful indifference. For his part, Reese saw a boy with shaggy dark blond hair that stuck up around the hat he wore. He was barefoot. His trousers torn in one knee. Reese guessed it would be a real challenge for his ma to keep him clean and tidy.

"You got a name?" the boy asked after a bit.

"Most people call me Reese."

"Huh. What do the others call you?"

Reese grinned. "Don't care what they call me so long as they don't call me late for dinner."

The boy nodded sagely. "Ain't that the truth?"

"You got a name?" Reese asked.

"My ma calls me Jimmy."

Reese decided to continue Jimmy's game. "What does your pa call you?"

"Ain't got no pa."

"Sorry to hear that."

"Ma says it weren't much of a loss when he died. She said he mostly spent his time gamblin' or drinkin'."

Reese sighed. "I know how that is. My pa was the same way. Though he was a good man when he stayed away from the strong drink."

"Yeah, what happened to him?"

"He got a little too drunk and fell in front of a wagon and got himself killed."

"Sorry to hear that."

Reese nodded. "Sorry to hear about your pa too."

"Where's your ma?"

"She's back in Chicago. Married again."

Jimmy dropped his foot to the ground and straightened. "You don't say. I don't think I'd care for my ma marryin' again, though I suppose she needs someone to take care of her."

Miss Victoria came around the corner. She paused. "Hi, Jimmy. Good day, Mr. Cartwright." She went inside before Reese could make it to his feet and speak to her.

Jimmy sighed. "She sure is a pretty lady. And nice too. You hear she wants to start a school? Ma says I'll have to go. I don't see no good reason for it. You don't need to read or write to farm or work in the livery stable, do ya?"

"I suppose not, though it helps to know what notices in the store say. And stuff like that."

Jimmy considered it a moment. "How long does it take to learn that much?"

"I can't rightly say." Reese shifted so he could see the screen door of the store. He caught a flicker of movement, like a skirt swinging. Or maybe it was only Mr. White moving something. He might have listened to hear if anything was said, but Jimmy was intent of discussing his education.

"I could go just long enough to learn that, I guess." He considered it a moment. "You think Miss Victoria is gonna be the teacher?"

"Well, I can't rightly say. Never thought about it. You think she'd make a good teacher?"

"Oh yeah. Once she told me about how the President of the United States bought a whole bunch of land from the French and Montana Territory was part of it. Then two guys called Lewis and Clark explored it with the help of some Indians. She made it sound real interestin'. Guess I wouldn't mind learnin' stuff like that."

So, she had received a good education just as she'd hinted at on Sunday. "It does sound interesting. Maybe I should go to school if she's teaching."

Jimmy whooped at the idea. "You're too old for schoolin'."

"Guess I might be. Besides, I bought a ranch, so I'll be busy." Reese stood and leaned his shoulder against the wall, hoping to see more of what was going on inside.

He might not have been as subtle as he hoped. "You hopin' to see more of Miss Victoria?"

"Me? Why do you ask?"

"'Cause you're tryin' to see inside. I'm guessin' she went in to see her friend Miss Walton, Mrs. White's sister, you know."

"I didn't, but then I'm new to town."

"I think they're plannin' somethin' for the show on Friday. I heard 'em practicin' some lines when they didn't know I was nearby."

The Friday event grew more and more inviting. But Reese hoped with a little diligence he might find an opportunity before then to speak to Victoria.

"You comin' Friday?" Jimmy asked.

"Sure plan to."

Jimmy leaned closer to whisper, "You want me to find out which box lunch is Miss Victoria's?"

It was an invitation Reese couldn't refuse. "I'd appreciate that."

"It's as good as done. I best get on home before Ma

comes lookin' for me." Jimmy jumped off the step and raced down the street, his dog trotting beside him.

Reese leaned against the wall, one booted foot tipped up. He meant to stay there until Victoria left the store.

* * *

"What are you doing?" Lisa's voice so close behind Victoria made her startle.

"Shh." She held her finger to her lips.

Lisa leaned around Victoria's shoulder. "Are you eavesdropping on Jimmy and whoever he is talking to?"

"I might be." Though she couldn't hear the conversation now with Lisa whispering to her.

"You know what they say. Eavesdroppers never hear anything good about themselves."

Victoria moved away from the door knowing she wouldn't hear anything more and would likely give away her presence to Reese. "That's where you're wrong. I heard good things."

They went to the back of the store to a little area Lisa's brother-in-law had set aside for the family to sit in when the store wasn't busy.

Lisa put her hands on her hips and faced Victoria. "Tell me what you heard."

Victoria had started listening even before she reached the store. As soon as she heard Reese's voice and realized he and Jimmy were talking, she had stayed out of sight around the corner of the store, overcome with curiosity.

"Jimmy and Mr. Cartwright have something in common. Both of them lost fathers who drank and gambled." The way the two had talked about their losses had tugged at something deep within Victoria. "At least they know what they lost. I don't even know that. Do I have family who wonders what's become of me?" Her parents had died in the train wreck that left Victoria the only survivor.

Lisa hugged her. "I'm sure you do."

"It's easy to say. But if I do, where are they? Why haven't they found me?" She lifted her arms in a gesture of impatience. "Oh, what does it matter? I am Victoria Kinsley now."

"Yes, you are. What else did you hear?"

Victoria chuckled. "Jimmy was telling him what a good teacher I was, and he said I had taught him about the Louisiana Purchase and the Lewis and Clark expedition. Honestly, I'm surprised he remembers a thing I said." She laughed again. "Mr. Cartwright said he should maybe go to school." She sobered. "It seems to me that Mr. Cartwright asks entirely too many questions about me."

"Why do you say that?"

"Why is he asking? Does he know me from before?"

"Do you have any reason to suspect he does?"

Victoria considered what she knew of the man and realized it was very little. "He says he's from Chicago." She caught Lisa's hand and shook her arm. "He looked at me like...like... Oh, I don't know. I suppose I'm being overly suspicious."

"Norm said Mr. Cartwright asked about you, but said he seemed interested in you as a woman, if you know what I mean?"

Victoria face went cold and she sank to the nearest chair. "That's not possible."

Lisa sat beside her. "Why not? You're a beautiful young woman. I can't say I blame Mr. Cartwright for wanting to get to know you better."

Victoria sucked in a strengthening breath. "But what if…"

"Victoria, are you going to spend your entire life wondering what if?"

"I can't help it."

"You ought to try. A handsome young man has asked about you. I expect he will want to see more of you. When he asks you to go walking with him or whatever he asks, why not say yes?"

"I'm afraid of my past."

"Maybe you'll never have a past. Only today and the rest of your life. Are you going to waste that? It seems to me you'll grow to regret such a choice."

"You make it sound so reasonable."

Lisa chuckled. "Maybe because I'm such a reasonable person."

Victoria laughed. "If you say so." Both of them knew Lisa didn't mind doing rash and wild things from time to time. And sometimes persuading Victoria to be part of it. "Remember skating on the river?" They'd found a quiet spot where it was frozen over, but the ice was not as thick as they thought.

Lisa shuddered. "We were fortunate to hear the cracking and get off the ice before it broke. But at least we won't repeat that mistake."

"So, you think Mr. Cartwright is only interested in courting me?"

"I do. And I think it's time you moved forward. Will you do that?"

Victoria considered the request. "I guess I can try."

"So, if he asks you to walk with him or whatever, you'll say yes?"

"Yes, okay. I'll say yes." Something fluttered in the pit of her stomach. For the first time in her memory, she considered embracing the future. Heaviness quickly replaced the fluttering. Since the day she'd wakened with no memory of who she was, she had felt as if the future could be snatched from her as easily as her past had been.

"Now let's practice for Friday night." Lisa's words allowed Victoria to push away her fears. Something she was adept at.

Sometime later, Victoria said goodbye to her friend. She paused before the door to look through the screen. Of course, he wasn't still there. Why did she think he would be? Lisa, with her romantic dreams, was causing her to have foolish thoughts.

She went out to the wooden step, turned right to return home, and almost plowed into Reese where he lounged against the wall, half hidden by the afternoon shadow.

"Oh. I didn't see you."

"Didn't mean to startle you." He unwound from the wall. "Are you going home?"

"Yes."

"May I walk you there?"

Her first instinct, born of years of guarding every association, was to say no, but she remembered her promise to her friend and wouldn't have been surprised if Lisa listened at the door. "That would be nice. Thank you."

He fell in at her side. "Jimmy was telling me how you taught him some history. He thinks a great deal of you."

"He's a good boy." She must be careful of what she said so as not to reveal that she had listened to Reese's conversation with Jimmy. "He lost his father before we came here. It's hard for him and his mother to manage, though people try to help them out."

"I lost my pa too, under similar circumstances."

She paused to look at him. "I'm sorry. How old were you?"

"I was fourteen, so older than young Jimmy. I was already working in the iron foundry in Chicago. Just like my pa. It was hard work. Are you familiar with a foundry?"

"Can't say that I am." She realized they had passed the intersection where they should have turned toward the manse. Was this Reese's way of spending time with her? Well, having agreed to accompany him, she let him lead the way.

"When my ma remarried after my pa died, I decided it was time for me to move on."

"I see. Was it because of your stepfather?"

"Mostly. But I'd never enjoyed the foundry work and, knowing Ma was going to be looked after, I was happy enough to leave. Just as they were happy to let me go."

"Doesn't it make you bitter?"

"I admit it hurt a little at the time but now I'm grateful. I have made arrangements to buy Abe Shaw's ranch and cattle, so I will soon be a rancher."

"It sounds like that's your dream come true."

"Guess you could say that." He didn't sound totally convinced but before she could ask him to explain, they reached the river where a bench had been placed so people could watch the water flow by. "Do you want to sit a spell?"

"That would be fine." They sat side by side.

"May I call you Victoria?" he asked.

"Yes, of course."

"And you must call me Reese."

"Thank you." What would he say if he knew she'd been calling him that in her mind since the first?

"Victoria, what's your dream?"

A jolt ran through her body. Her fingers curled. *To know who I am*, she silently wailed. But she could not say so knowing how self-pitying it sounded. "I'm adopted. All the Kinsley girls are. There are six of us. Tilly and Adele stayed back in Verdun, Ohio. Adele is married with a young son. Tilly is working for a well-to-do family. Then there's Josh. He was born to the family, but we haven't seen nor heard from him in almost two years." She wondered if he, too, had had an accident and lost his memory. "It's why we moved west. You see, he'd gone west, and we're hoping to locate him." Trying to find Josh made her realize what a difficult job it would be for someone to try and find her. Except she'd been a youngster. Maybe fourteen or fifteen. Shouldn't any family have known where to look for her? Which brought her back to the only conclusion she could draw. She understood her parents had died in the crash and, other than them, she had no family. Or at least no family who wanted anything to do with her. She had often considered scenarios to explain the latter. Her mother had married against her family's wishes and so was estranged from the rest of the family. Or her mother had run away from her family and they didn't know anything about Victoria. Or the worst, the one she prayed was false. She'd been born out of wedlock and her mother's parents had disowned them. And her father didn't even know about her.

"I had heard that you are adopted. The Kinsleys have given you a good home."

"Yes, they have and I'm grateful especially—" Her breath shuddered. "They don't know anything about me."

He shifted to study her face. "That doesn't seem unusual. Aren't many orphaned children abandoned without any knowledge of their family?"

She nodded. "Like Adele. She was left on their doorstep as a baby. Flora and Eve's parents died. Josie came when she was twelve. She knew her family. I came when I was older. Maybe fourteen or fifteen, but I have no knowledge of my family."

His eyebrows went up. His eyes widened. "How can that be?"

"I was injured in a train accident. I was the only survivor. My parents were killed in the accident. I was unconscious for three days and when I came to, I had no memory of who I was." Cold vibrated through her. "No one came looking for me." Her teeth chattered.

"Amnesia. Four years of it. That's incredible." He shook his head, as if the idea was too far-fetched to be believable. Then he looked at her more closely. "You're shaking." He touched her hand. "You're cold as ice. Come on, I'll take you home." He pulled her to her feet.

Her legs wobbled. She couldn't walk, could barely stand, and she grabbed his arm for support. She should never have told him her story. It left her weak and frightened.

When she first came to in the hospital, she had looked intently into every face she saw, hoping for a sign of recognition. She'd cried when no one offered to tell her about herself.

Now she feared someone would come along and snatch her from her happy life.

But at the moment, all she wanted was to get home, crawl into her bed, pull the covers over her head, and stay there.

## CHAPTER 3

Reese had his arms about Victoria's shoulders and held her upright as they made their way to the manse. It was bold of him to touch her so intimately, but she shook so badly she couldn't stand without his assistance.

Amnesia! Was it possible? Victoria certainly seemed affected by relating the story. The pain in her voice at telling him no one had come looking for her was real enough to sting his own heart. However, it didn't make sense. And claiming her parents were dead. Reese knew they certainly had not been killed in a train accident. Mr. Hayworth had searched far and wide. He'd questioned everyone in the foundry, including Reese, who was only sixteen. His questions were so severe that Reese had felt he'd been accused of abducting the girl. Indeed, the man's suspicions grew with each passing day making Reese even more anxious to leave the foundry. Perhaps Mr. Hayworth had seen Reese watching his daughter that day he walked by their house and considered him a likely suspect. Finding Constance Hayworth would effectively prove the man wrong.

Mr. Hayworth had offered a generous reward for any information regarding his missing daughter. It wasn't possible that the girl had been overlooked. But it seemed too much of a coincidence to think Victoria was in an accident and lost her memory at the same time the Hayworth girl disappeared. Victoria was well educated. More so than the other Kinsley girls.

He would write a long-overdue letter to his mother and ask if Miss Hayworth had been found.

He reached the manse and opened the back door without knocking.

Mrs. Kinsley turned from tending something on the stove, took one look at Victoria, and flew to Reese's side. "Victoria, child, what has happened?"

Victoria rolled her head back and forth, her teeth rattling together.

"Josie, Eve, come quickly," Mrs. Kinsley called. "And bring some blankets." Footsteps clattered down the stairs as Reese and her mother eased Victoria to a chair that Reese dragged close to the stove.

The girls rushed into the room, saw their sister, and wrapped blankets about her, making soothing noises.

Mrs. Kinsley poured some water into the kettle and set it to boil. She put a handful of tea leaves in a brown pot. Then she knelt before Victoria while she waited for the kettle to boil. "Child, what is wrong?"

"I don't know." Victoria's tight whisper carried an ocean full of tears.

Her mother rose and faced Reese. "Tell me what happened."

"We went for a walk to the river and she was telling me about the family. She told me about being adopted. About having amnesia." His throat grew tight.

He drew Mrs. Kinsley away and bent close to whisper. "It was when she told me that no one came to find her that she got like this."

The woman nodded and patted his hand. "That explains it. Thank you for bringing her home. You're welcome to stay for supper." She made tea and held a cupful to Victoria's lips.

"Drink this, my child. You know you will always have a home with us. We love you and cherish you as our daughter." Josie and Eve huddled close to her, murmuring words of love and comfort.

Reese hovered nearby watching Victoria. Her shock was real enough. But how was it possible? Instead of getting answers to his questions, he ended up with more questions.

Victoria's hands steadied. "I'm all right now."

Her mother and sisters remained clustered around her.

She smiled at each of them. "Thank you." She saw Reese, and her smile faltered. "I'm sorry to be such a nuisance but thank you for bringing me home."

"No reason to apologize."

She held his gaze a moment, seeking, searching…for what, he couldn't say. He knew how essential knowing the truth and believing it was to her peace of mind. Perhaps the letter to his ma would settle the matter once and for all about whether or not she was the missing Hayworth girl. But if she wasn't, then who was she? For her sake he wished he could provide the answer.

The young widow Reese had met on Sunday entered the house, her two children racing in ahead of her. It took him a moment to recall her name. Stella Norwood. The boy, Donny, five years old, if Reese recalled correctly, saw Reese and planted himself in front of him.

"You were here afore."

"On Sunday, yes."

"How come you're back? It's not Sunday."

"Donny, mind your manners," his mother said. "I apologize," she said to Reese.

At seeing a stranger in the house, little Blossom clung shyly to her mother's side. Again, Reese struggled to recall what he'd been told. The blonde child was three years old, he thought someone had said.

Reese chuckled at Donny's question. "I take it that Sunday is the day for company."

"Mostly," Donny said.

"Well, it so happens I was at the store and so was Miss Victoria, so I walked her home."

Stella, from her chair by the table, glanced from Victoria to Reese, her expression full of interest.

Reese pretended not to notice the questioning look in her eyes.

Victoria shrugged from the blankets and got to her feet. "It's getting on to suppertime." She went to the stove and stirred the pot her mother had been tending.

Josie folded the blankets and took them away.

Eve started to peel potatoes.

"I can do that," Stella said, and took over the job, but she remained seated as she worked.

The women were soon busy, leaving Reese to stand

by, feeling about as useless as a cold stove. "What can I do?"

Four women turned to look at him.

"I've been known to help my mother when I lived at home. And I know how to make a few things as a matter of survival."

It was Victoria who asked the question that surely all the others thought. "Exactly what do you make?"

He grinned, pleased to be able to provide an answer that would surprise them. "Baking powder biscuits is my specialty."

"Then by all means." She pointed him toward the flour bin and the other ingredients he'd need.

Aware that they all, including Donny and Blossom, covertly watched his every more, he measured out what he needed, chopped in lard, mixed in milk to make a batter the right consistency. He rolled out and cut biscuits and put them on a baking tray. The potatoes were already cooking so he judged it time to bake the biscuits and slid the tray into the oven.

He stood back and dusted his hands, feeling rather pleased with himself. He glanced around at the others, who suddenly looked very busy. "Surprised you all some, didn't I?"

Victoria chuckled. "Are you gloating?"

"A little. Am I allowed?"

Mrs. Kinsley patted his shoulder. "You've impressed me, and I have to admit that doesn't happen often."

He laughed and looked around at the others.

The girls looked at each other and grinned.

Stella hugged her children close. "I'm going to teach both these young ones to cook basics."

The preacher entered and everyone greeted him. He bent to kiss his wife then looked at Reese. "See you came back." He studied Reese a moment. "Got your eye on one of the girls?"

"Hush, now," Mrs. Kinsley said. "He brought Victoria home. She was in quite a state."

The preacher went to Victoria. "What happened?"

Victoria brushed aside her parents' concerns. "It was all so foolish. I assure you it won't happen again."

Her parents exchanged a look that Reese wished he understood. He hated to think ill of these good people, but were they hiding Victoria? And for what reason?

Nothing about this situation made any sense. Besides writing to his mother, he meant to spend time with the family and especially with Victoria until he learned the truth. The truth would set them all free.

Or would it rob them of the joy and peace they had at the moment?

\* \* \*

Victoria did her best to avoid looking at Reese over supper, but it was difficult with him sitting directly across from her. It didn't help that Donny asked a hundred questions about cows and horses and Reese answered kindly.

"I want to be a rancher," Donny said, his voice firm, as if the matter was settled.

"If your mother approves, I'll take you to see my ranch."

"Ma, Ma. Can I?"

Victoria chuckled at Donny's eagerness, and she met

Reese's eyes across the table. Such dark eyes that offered a world of—

*Victoria, don't be foolish. Just because he brought you home. And he's kind to a little boy.*

But something about having him bring her home struck a deeply buried chord. She knew instantly what it was. The idea of returning home. She thought she'd laid all those hopes and disappointments to rest. She did not wish to have them resurrected. Home was here. As Victoria Kinsley.

"I think you may," Stella said.

"When? When?" Donny bounced up and down on his chair.

"I can't say for sure but soon. I promise, and I won't forget."

Those words echoed in Victoria's head and stayed there. *I promise, and I won't forget.*

Forgetting was far too easy. Easier than remembering.

Again, she tried to ignore him, but his biscuits were light as a cloud, and she had to add her praise to that of the others. "You certainly know how to make good biscuits."

"Thank you. It's one of my many talents."

"Good to know. Which makes me think of the talent show on Friday. Perhaps you have a talent you can share with us. A quarter for the entry fee and it's all for a good cause."

He studied her perhaps not more than a fraction of a second, and yet she felt as if time had ceased to exist. "I'll give it some thought."

Josie sat beside him and nudged his elbow. "I can't wait to see what you come up with."

"Nor can I," he said with such dryness that everyone laughed.

He hung around after the meal ended, insisting he'd help with the dishes. "Another of my talents," he said. "Do you suppose I could do that for the talent show?"

"I might pay an extra quarter to watch that," Victoria said, and the girls laughed.

It was her turn to wash and Reese grabbed a towel, prepared to dry.

"You're so handy in the kitchen you won't need a wife," she said. Where had those words come from? It sounded like she regretted the fact that he had said he didn't plan to marry. Hopefully he wouldn't notice, though she couldn't begin to hope Josie and Eve hadn't. She knew she was correct when they looked at each other and grinned.

"A wife is a handy thing to have. Saves a man much time in the kitchen. Why, I've heard it said, a good wife can turn a house into a home." He spoke solemnly as if talking about a new kitchen gadget and earned himself hoots of laughter and derision from the others.

Victoria kept her attention on scrubbing the potato pot. For the first time in her memory, she allowed herself to think what it would be like to be a wife. She had Lisa to thank for her wayward thoughts and she would scold her friend the next time they were together.

The kitchen was clean. Ma and Pa had gone to the parlor. Stella had taken her children to bed. Victoria knew she wouldn't come back out. The poor woman was still as weak as a newborn kitten.

Reese reached for his hat.

Josie caught his elbow. "Don't be in a hurry to go. Come with us to the church. We like to play the piano and sing."

He tucked his hat under his arm. "Sounds good."

Josie and Eve rushed out the door, leaving Victoria to escort Reese next door.

"I thank you again for bringing me home safely this afternoon." Again, the words—home and safety—tugged at her insides. She pushed them away. She had a home right here where she was loved and cared for.

"Was it talking about not having any memory that upset you?"

"I guess. You have no idea how unsettling it is to wonder who you are. To see strangers and fear they will know you, but you won't know them."

"I don't know, of course, but I expect it can be quite frightening."

"I've had amnesia so long I am now afraid of getting my memory back. The chances are if I do, I will forget all this." Her insides began to quiver. "The doctor warned me that regaining my long-term memory made it entirely possible I might forget the memories I've made during the duration of my amnesia. I don't want to lose what I have. And yet I wish I knew who I really am."

Reese touched her arm. "Don't upset yourself about it. Remember the verse you told me. 'As the mountains are round about Jerusalem, so the Lord is round about his people from henceforth even for ever.' Think of God surrounding you with His arms and His love. I have another verse for you. I read it just last night. It's Isaiah 41, verse ten. I won't quote the whole of it. You can look it up if you want to know what else it says. 'Fear thou not; for I am with thee: be not dismayed. I will help thee. I will uphold thee.'"

They had stopped walking and faced each other. She looked into his steady, dark gaze, and found strength and encouragement. As much from him as from the words he spoke. "Thank you. I will remember those words every time I get worried and fearful."

"Are you two coming?" Josie called from the church.

With a little self-conscious laugh, Victoria hurried on, Reese at her side.

By the time they stepped into the interior, Eve was playing the piano and Josie standing at the pulpit singing. She beckoned them forward.

Not knowing if Reese would be familiar with the words of the hymns that all the Kinsleys knew by heart, Victoria took a hymnal from a pew as she marched up the aisle.

She and Reese stood beside Eve and sang hymn after hymn. Reese joined in on the songs he was familiar with. He had a deep bass voice that added to the different parts they sang.

After a bit, Josie left the piano and Eve took her place. "We all play the piano," Victoria explained to Reese. "Ma made sure of that, though she didn't have to teach me. I already knew how to play."

Josie stood beside Victoria. "She plays better than any of us. Funny how she remembers that and not who she is."

Strange indeed, Victoria thought. They sang some more, and she gave herself over to enjoying the music and Reese's voice blending with hers and her sisters'.

Eve stopped playing and came to the pulpit. "It's your turn."

Victoria sat at the piano. As soon as she began to play, everything else faded away as she lost herself in the music. At the end of the piece, she glanced up to see Reese watching her, his eyes dark with an emotion she couldn't identify.

Josie and Eve nudged each other as they watched him.

She wanted to tell them it wasn't that. In fact, if she had to guess, she'd say he was measuring her, assessing her. Was he seeing her as someone without a past?

"Come and join me, Eve," Victoria said, and her sister sat beside her on the piano bench. They played a duet. They played faster and faster, the goal to see who would stumble first. They both lifted their hands at the same time and laughed.

"I have an idea for the talent show," Josie said.

Eve and Victoria grinned at each other. "See how fast we can play that piece?"

"That might be fun too. But what about a quartet? Us and Reese."

Reese blinked. Opened his mouth and closed it without saying anything.

Eve pressed the matter. "You did say you wanted to do something for the talent show."

He studied each of them a moment and a slow, heart-stopping smile came to his face. "Okay, let's do it." He and Josie moved to stand behind Eve and Victoria at the piano bench. They flipped through the hymnal looking for something that suited them all.

Finally, they settled on one, and Victoria was chosen

to be the accompanist. The others crowded to her back as they practiced.

"We do sound good together," she said when they were reasonably satisfied with their progress.

"Let's get together tomorrow evening and go over it again," Eve said.

Everyone agreed. Victoria wanted to refuse. There was something about Reese that unsettled her. It could be his dark good looks, or the memory of having turned into a quivering mess in his presence, or simply that she didn't feel free to embrace a future of any shape. This had all started with agreeing to let him walk her home. She would make sure Lisa realized what she'd gotten Victoria into with that promise to say yes to an invitation from Reese.

They parted ways at the manse, Reese to the livery barn where he said he had picked up a few days' work. "Need some cash to buy supplies," he explained.

The girls went inside. Ma and Pa were sitting at the table drinking tea and discussing Pa's sermon notes for the following Sunday. It was a time when the parents liked to be alone, so the girls said good night and went upstairs to prepare for bed.

As usual, Victoria sat at the writing table by the window, opened her latest journal, and began to write in it. Her sisters knew the reason for her meticulous detailing of her day.

She'd explained it many times. "I don't know my past, don't know what the future holds, but I don't want to forget one moment of right now. No matter what happens, I'll be able to read about it and remember." Her throat tightened now as she considered the possibility.

"Vicki." Eve caught her attention. "What happened to bring you home in such a state this afternoon?"

"Yeah, you scared us," Josie added.

"It was so strange. I was telling Reese about the family. How all the girls are adopted. Then I told him about me losing my memory. I don't know what came over me but when I told about how no one came looking for me, I got cold and started to shake."

"Oh Vick, you poor thing." Both girls came to her side and hugged her. "You are one of us now, and I hope you always will be," Eve said.

Victoria bent her cheek to first one sister then the other. "You know, this is all Lisa's fault."

The girls sat back on their heels to stare at Victoria.

"Yes. She said I needed to forget my lost past and go boldly into the future. Well, those weren't her exact words, but that's what she meant. Then she made me promise to say yes if Reese asked to accompany me on a walk. I promised, so when he asked me, I was honor bound to agree."

Eve and Josie grinned at each other.

"I'm sure it was a terrible hardship," Eve said.

"I don't know how you endured it." Josie could barely get the words out before she laughed.

"I quite enjoyed myself," Victoria said, doing her best to sound superior.

The three of them laughed and Victoria picked up her pen to write.

Eve and Josie hung over her shoulders.

Victoria pulled her journal away. "This is private."

The pair nudged each other and winked as they made their way to their respective beds.

"It's private," Josie whispered loudly.

"Private," Eve echoed, and they laughed.

Victoria laughed too. She didn't mind being teased. It was part of being loved. She mused over what to write in her journal. She never hid her writings and didn't mind if others read her description of the day but to her knowledge, no one ever did though sometimes they asked her to read parts aloud. She bent her head and wrote several pages then blotted the ink dry. Just before she closed the book, Eve begged her to read about the day.

She turned to face them and started reading about the chores they had done in the morning.

"Skip to when you were at the store," Eve said.

She did so, not leaving out anything—not how she'd eavesdropped on Reese and Jimmy, nor how Lisa had said Reese's interest in her was as a man wanting to court a woman. When she got to the part about sitting on the bench, the other girls sighed.

"It's so romantic," Josie said.

"You know the rest. You were there." Victoria closed the book.

Eve sat up. "You didn't read how you got home. You can't skip that."

So, with a pretend, long-suffering groan, she read those words then slipped into bed where she lay beside Josie, her eyes closed, pretending she had fallen asleep. But sleep eluded her as her thoughts swirled round and round with an unsettling mix of fear and hope.

Hope that she could embrace the future.

Fear that her past would come back and destroy the world she knew and loved.

## CHAPTER 4

Reese fought a battle with himself all the next day. He only wanted to get close to Victoria to discover the truth about her. He didn't want to care for her. More and more he suspected she was really Constance Hayworth.

Determined to get to the truth of the matter, he wrote a letter to his mother and posted it that morning. Soon he would know if Miss Hayworth had been returned to the bosom of her family.

If not, then there was a good chance Victoria was the missing girl. If so, she was the daughter of a rich man who could appear on the scene any moment and snatch her away. He surely didn't want any part of that. Not when she appeared so happy and content as Victoria Kinsley.

He should stay away from the Kinsleys until he heard back from his mother.

Unfortunately, he couldn't deny a strange and powerful urge to protect her from the likes of Smitty and anyone else who might realize who she was. Besides, he'd agreed to sing a song with the three Kinsley sisters so had to meet them at the church later.

He did his best to occupy his day at the livery barn. He cleaned the stalls, swept the floors, and even washed the window in the little office. Then he removed a plank that had been damaged and set about replacing it with a new one.

Jimmy came by in the afternoon. "Miss Victoria is at the store again if you want to go walk her home like ya did yesterday."

Reese turned from fixing a gate to stare at the boy. "How do you know I walked her home?"

"I saw you. Took her by way of the river, didn't cha?"

"Jimmy, my friend, you better be careful who you spy on. It could land you in a heap of trouble."

"Only if I'm caught."

"You be careful, hear?"

"Always am. You gonna go to the store now?"

"Not this time. Mickey is away on some business and expects me to take care of this place."

Jimmy slouched and scuffed his toe in the dirt.

"Why does it matter so much to you?"

"She's nice and pretty and you're handsome and nice. I just thought..." His voice trailed off.

Reese hooted. "Jimmy, I never thought to see you in the role of matchmaker."

"Why not? I asked Ma about it and she said Miss Victoria was the perfect age for gettin' married. How about you? Aren't you the right age?"

"I'm twenty. Can't rightly say if that's the right age or not."

"Sounds like a good age to me. Miss Victoria is eighteen."

Reese knew that though he wondered how the Kinsleys had come to know her correct age. Another fact that made him wonder where the truth lay. "How do you know?"

"I asked her friend, Miss Lisa, at the store. She said Miss Victoria was maybe eighteen, but she wasn't sure. 'How can ya not be sure?' I asked. All she said was sometimes you aren't. Funny, huh?"

Not so funny as much as sad, confusing, and suspicious, but Reese kept his thoughts to himself.

Jimmy hung around about another hour, entertaining Reese with his view on town life. When he left, suddenly remembering he was running an errand for his mother, Reese chuckled to himself. The scamp knew the comings and goings of most people in town and had an opinion on everything.

Toward supper time, Mickey returned from his business and Reese sauntered over to Sylvie's Diner. Sylvie, he'd discovered, was a rotund little woman with a thick bun of graying hair and a loud voice.

"You got two options on the menu," she said the first time he put in an appearance. "I only make one item. Your choice is take it or leave it."

Reese had chuckled. "I'll take it. By the way, what is it?"

"Roast beef and everything that goes with it," Sylvie said, and brought in a plate piled high with food. The aroma brought a flood of saliva to Reese's mouth.

"And apple pie, if I think you deserve it."

"Apple pie? What do I have to do to deserve it?" He

scooped up a forkful of fluffy mashed potatoes drowned in rich brown gravy.

Sylvie sat across from him. "I heard you been squiring Miss Victoria home from the store. You can tell me what your intentions are toward her."

He stared at her. "Isn't that a question her pa should ask?"

"Miss Victoria is a special young lady. I might not be her ma, but I care about her and I don't want to see her hurt. So, are your intentions honorable?"

Reese bought himself a little time by tackling the plate of food. "Good meal."

"Uh huh." She clearly didn't mean to budge from the spot without getting an answer from him. And Reese guessed it better be an answer that pleased her.

"I was at the store when she left and asked if she wanted me to walk her home."

"The river is out of your way."

"So, we took the scenic route." His food was quickly losing flavor. Was there no such thing as privacy in this town?

"You're skirting my question. What is your intention?"

He leaned forward and grinned at Sylvie. "I've been in town five days. Hardly time for me to have much in the way of intentions." He sobered. "The only thing I can tell you is I mean to always be honest about my feelings." He returned his attention to his food. It turned the green beans bitter to know he wasn't being entirely honest with Victoria about other things. But then, what could he say? That he thought she looked like someone he'd seen in the past…the past she had forgotten? It hardly seemed the thing to make her anxious to see him again, especially given the way she'd reacted to telling him about losing her memory.

Sylvie sniffed. "That girl is something special, and I expect you to remember it."

"Don't seem I'm likely to forget it with you keeping an eye on things."

She snorted. "You can count on it. Now, you still want that pie?"

"You mean I deserve it?"

"That has yet to be seen." She marched away and returned with a slice that was a quarter of a large pie. If this is what she gave to a person she wasn't sure deserved it, he couldn't imagine the size given to someone she approved of.

He glanced at the clock hanging by the kitchen door. It was about time to make his way to the church. "Thanks for the meal. And the warning." He handed over the coins for his food and sauntered down the street toward the church. He was sure eyes peered at him from every window and little boys peeked around every corner.

By the time he reached the church, he chuckled softly.

Not seeing anyone else there, he slipped inside.

"You sound amused."

He started at Victoria's voice nearby and slid into the pew beside her. "I hope you know there are people in town ready to defend you from people who might hurt you." He told her that Jimmy and Sylvie knew about their walk. "I've been duly warned." He shuddered. "Miss Sylvie scares me."

Victoria laughed, a sound that rivaled Sunday morning bells.

She stopped so suddenly he glanced about to see the cause.

"What were you warned about?" she asked.

He tried to think how to explain it without making it sound like he meant to seriously court her. He didn't. Not after Betty, who pretended one thing while being something else entirely. Victoria? She might not be pretending, but if she turned out to be the missing rich girl, all it would take for her to be spirited away was someone contacting Mr. Hayworth. Someone like Smitty. "She was very clear that she expects you to be treated in a special fashion."

"And what did you say to that?"

"Yes, ma'am." He gave a smart salute that earned him a burst of laughter. "What else could I say? She serves the best restaurant meal in town."

"She serves the *only* restaurant meal in town."

"All the more reason to agree to anything she says."

Victoria studied him unblinkingly, her blue eyes full of dark depths.

He steeled himself to return look for look. He couldn't answer her unasked questions any more than he could say what they were. He couldn't give Sylvie the assurance she wanted. Or explain to himself what he wanted.

Sure, he wanted to make sure Victoria was okay. That meant sticking around in case Smitty came back, because he was sure the man would return. Then Reese's task would be to convince him not to think of Victoria as the missing Constance Hayworth. At least not until he knew if the Hayworth girl was still missing.

He knew he had to protect her from the likes of

Smitty if for no other reason than he had blurted out her likeness to the missing girl. Protecting her was the right thing to do.

He'd considered all possibilities for the mystery of who she was.

One, she might truly not have any memory.

Or she might be pretending for reasons of her own.

Or the Kinsleys had somehow influenced her.

But the one that caused him the most concern was that someone wished her harm and she was hiding.

Victoria gave a triumphant smile. "Then I shall expect to be treated in a special fashion."

He saluted. "Yes, ma'am."

They laughed together.

Josie and Eve rushed through the door and skidded to a stop.

"What's so funny?"

"Tell us the joke."

Reese sighed. "'Tis the worst town ever for everyone knowing everyone else's business."

Victoria laughed so hard she had to wipe tears away and Reese grinned, feeling rather proud of his ability to amuse her.

Her sisters looked less pleased with him. He quickly explained. "If you must know, I was telling how Miss Sylvie threatened to refuse me a piece of pie if I didn't treat Victoria right. I'm sure she meant all of you," he added hastily lest they take offense.

Eve and Josie joined arms and faced him. "What have you been doing to earn Sylvie's warning?"

"Oh, good grief." He looked to the ceiling as if appealing for help in that direction.

"He isn't going to help you." Josie sounded quite certain that Reese couldn't expect godly intervention.

Victoria chuckled at Reese's predicament then got to her feet and pushed him from between the pews. "Come on, you two. Stop picking on him. We're supposed to be practicing."

Victoria laughed as she urged him onward, while the other two muttered as they followed. Reese couldn't believe he was part of such a scene and turned to face them.

"I'm sure glad Miss Sylvie can't see how you're all treating me. No, wait. I think if I tell her she'll give me a really big piece of pie." He smacked his lips. "With a mound of whipped cream. Yummy."

He led the laughing procession to the front of the church and swept a bow to Victoria to sit at the bench. He crowded in beside her, raising his eyebrows as he turned to the other two girls.

"According to Miss Sylvie, it is my duty to see that Victoria is treated right."

The three of them pushed him right off the bench. He dusted himself off. "I'm going to have to tell Miss Sylvie about this, you know."

Victoria began to play, a bouncy little tune he didn't recognize.

He stood behind her, Eve and Josie at his sides, and listened. Victoria ended that tune and sighed.

"They say music calms the savage beast. I know it soothes me when I'm upset." She glanced over her shoulder at the three standing behind her. "I hope you have all settled down so we can get serious about practice."

Reese saluted. "Yes, ma'am." He succeeded in getting her to laugh again then she shook her head and began to play the song they meant to present at the talent night.

He'd always enjoyed singing but usually the cows were his only audience. Sometimes they joined in with a note or two, but they didn't sound a tenth as good as the Kinsley sisters.

His sudden laugh broke the rehearsal, and three girls stared at him.

"I'm sorry." He held up his hands. "I was thinking how I normally only sing around cows and am accompanied by their plaintive moos and an occasional bellow. I decided this is better."

Victoria shook her head. "I think that is the first time I've been compared to a cow."

Eve sighed. "Me too, but at least he was kind enough to say we're better."

Josie lifted her hands in a sign of resignation. "You can take the cowboy from the cows, but you can't take the cow out of the cowboy."

It was several seconds before they all sobered up enough to continue practice.

* * *

THAT NIGHT, Victoria had much to write in her journal. She couldn't remember the last time she'd laughed so often or so hard. She chuckled as she wrote down the events of the day, though mostly she wrote about the evening.

"Why do you think Sylvie felt she had to warn him?" Eve asked.

"Because she favors Victoria," Josie said.

"She does not." Victoria felt she had to deny it even though she knew it was true.

"Yes, she does, and has ever since you found her in her room, sick with a cold, and took over the restaurant for a week. She says you saved her life and her business."

"I just happened to be there at the right time."

"Vic, you deserve her praise. You did a good thing." Eve's tone was gentle.

"You're not jealous?"

"Of course not." Both of them answered as one.

Josie sat up on her elbow. "You deserve every good thing that comes your way. Including Reese."

Victoria tossed a pillow at her. "He's nice enough and makes me laugh but that's as far as it goes."

"For now," Eve said. "Read us what you wrote."

Victoria did so and the girls laughed again. Thanks to her careful notes, this would be one day she would enjoy over and over no matter what the future held.

THE NEXT MORNING the girls were busy decorating baskets for the box social and speculating as to who would buy their lunch and, along with the food, the privilege of sharing it with them.

"I think Reese will buy yours," Josie said.

"How will he know which one is mine?" If Reese bought her lunch at least she wouldn't be forced to share with a stranger and wonder if he knew her from her previous life.

Reese had given no indication that he knew her, so she didn't have that concern.

"A man who is interested has his ways of finding out." Josie and Eve grinned at each other.

"You can't tell him."

"Of course not." Eve looked duly sincere.

Victoria looked from one sister to the other. "Don't push me at him. Or him at me." A shiver raced across her shoulders. "I don't know if I'll ever be able to face strangers without fearing they know me from before. And if they do, what do they know? It's very unsettling."

The girls relented. "I wish you didn't have that worry," Eve said.

Josie hugged Victoria. "I wish you could know who you are without forgetting us." They all sniffled. Her sisters knew her concern that the return of her memory would erase any memory of being a Kinsley.

Eve returned to preparing her basket. "I don't like the feeling that a huge anvil is hanging over you, over all of us, and none of us knows when it will fall. Can't even run from it."

Sobered by the thought, Victoria returned to her task though the anticipation was dulled by the continual threat of that anvil.

After they had dinner, Stella and the children retreated to their room for a nap.

Ma watched them leave. "I had hoped Stella would be getting her strength back by now. But I tend to forget she almost died." She picked up her knitting. Ma always had socks and mittens on the go, as well as sweaters and scarves, most of which she gave to those who came to them sick, injured, or down on their luck.

"Lisa and I are planning something for the talent show. I need to go practice." Victoria left the house and decided she was early so would take a leisurely stroll. Which just happened to take her by the livery stable.

She slowed as she approached the barn. Jimmy and his dog came into view. Jimmy waved his arms as if describing something big and wonderful.

Victoria took two more steps and saw that Jimmy talked to Reese who curried a horse.

Reese's shoulders shook as he laughed at something Jimmy said. His hat shaded his face so she couldn't see his eyes, but his mouth was visible. She smiled to think of the laughter they had shared.

She stayed close to the buildings ,so she wasn't observed by Jimmy or Reese and took two more steps. She knew it was wrong to eavesdrop, but nevertheless she hoped to overhear their conversation. Her foot dislodged a stone and it rattled down the street.

Jimmy leaned back. "It's Miss Victoria. Hi."

"Hi yourself." She gave up trying to be invisible. "How are you? Oh hi, Reese." As if she was surprised to see him!

"I'm good." Jimmy rocked back and forth. "Tomorrow is the talent show. And boxed lunch. Ma is going to make a lunch. I'm thinkin' I'll buy it." He stuck his hand in his trouser pocket and jingled a few coins. "I been runnin' errands to earn a little money for that purpose." He studied Reese. "I could brush the horse for you. I could do them all. You might think it's worth a nickel."

Reese chuckled and adjusted Jimmy's crooked hat. "I'll gladly let you brush all the horses for a quarter." He handed Jimmy the curry comb and Jimmy took over the job.

Reese leaned back on the fence, his arms outspread

on the top rail. Victoria rested her elbows on the same rail to watch Jimmy. Her elbow brushed his wrist.

A jolt of warmth raced to her heart and it was all she could do not to jerk away and draw attention to the innocent barely-there touch.

"He reminds me of myself at that age," Reese said, forcing Victoria to shepherd her thoughts back to the boy. And the man who was speaking.

"How's that?" She couldn't picture him a ragged little boy.

"For one thing, I lived in town. Chicago." He paused as if asking if she remembered.

"You've said you lived there."

"I often went to the nearby barn to help with the horses. I ran up and down the streets and alleys. I suppose I saw a lot of things others didn't, just like young Jimmy here." He chuckled. "I have a feeling there isn't much goes on in Glory without him knowing."

"His ma has her hands full trying to make a living. She does laundry. A back-breaking job if ever there was one. The poor woman's hands are sometimes raw from scrubbing."

They watched Jimmy eagerly doing his job.

Reese tipped his hat back, letting the sun illuminate his face. "I'd like to say he needs a new pa but there's no guarantee that wouldn't make things worse for him."

"And he's too young to leave home like you did."

"I'll have to ask Sylvie to watch out for him." Reese's tone was so solemn she thought he truly meant to do exactly that. Then she realized he was joshing, and she laughed.

"I doubt that Sylvie needs to be told to do so. She

likely checks out every unmarried man who comes to town. Not to mention every resident and visitor." Victoria gave him a considering look. He turned and met her gaze.

"What?"

"My pa is measuring you for a wedding suit." She blushed to think Reese might think she was fishing for more attention from him. She rushed on to add, "And Miss Sylvie is watching your every step. Even Jimmy has his eye on you. I'd say it was enough to keep you living very carefully."

He laughed. "At least at my ranch I can hope for a little privacy."

"Apart from cows who help you sing?"

His eyes warmed and a smile settled into them. "What they lack in musical talent, they make up for in total disinterest."

Expecting him to say enthusiasm, his choice of words struck her as funny and she laughed.

"I'm done," Jimmy called. "Guess I'll do the next one." He trotted away.

"Oh goodness. I've forgotten the time. Lisa and I are practicing for the talent show. She'll be wondering where I am." Victoria lifted her skirts and took three steps.

"Wait. I'll walk you over." Reese vaulted over the fence and fell in at her side.

They walked up the street and turned left. White's store was at the far end of the street. A wagon rumbled past. The driver waved.

"Mr. Marsh," she said by way of explanation. "He and his family are homesteaders." She wondered if Reese objected to the homesteaders as many ranchers did. "Pa says what he lacks in experience he makes up for with dogged determination."

He chuckled at her echo of his comment.

A pair of cowboys rode by and touched the brim of their hats in greeting.

"Those two have been to dinner on Sundays."

A couple emerged from the hotel. Strangers. Her footsteps faltered.

Reese stopped. "Something wrong?"

"I don't know those people." She couldn't keep the tremor from her voice.

Reese studied her. "Is that a problem?"

Of course, he thought her reaction odd. "It's simply that every time I see a stranger, I wonder if they know me even though I don't know them. It's an unsettling feeling."

He drew her arm around his. "I expect it is, but they are showing no interest in you." He guided her up the street to the store.

The door opened and Miss Sylvie stepped out with a basket of purchases. She looked at Victoria's arm entwined with Reese's then gave Reese a forbidding look. "Humph." She tossed her head, sending the strings of her bonnet into a mad dance and hurried past them.

Victoria withdrew her arm. "She doesn't sound impressed. I hope she isn't going to refuse to feed you."

Reese pressed a hand to his stomach. "I hope not too, but I can always make biscuits." His gaze held hers.

Why did she think she saw things in his eyes that she had no business believing? Things like hope, promise, safety...

Stop. How could she hope she would ever be safe from her past?

"Lisa will be waiting for me."

"I'll see you later." He waited for her to step inside. She watched through the door as he walked away. She lifted her hand in quick goodbye just as he turned and touched the brim of his hat.

"Now what are you doing?" Lisa's voice, so close behind her, made her jump.

"You have to stop sneaking up on me. You're going to turn my hair gray."

Lisa leaned against her side and looked out the door. "Oh, so that's it."

"That's what?" She feigned confusion.

"That handsome cowboy I've been hearing so much about."

Victoria stepped back. "Not from me."

"Jimmy gave me a detailed account of your walk by the river and singing at the church."

Victoria rolled her eyes.

"And Miss Sylvie just left. She has a lot to say about Mr. Cartwright."

"It's just as Reese says. Nothing in this town is private."

"Should it be?" Lisa waggled her eyebrows. "Is there something you aren't telling me?"

"If there is, I'm sure Jimmy of Sylvie or a dozen others will inform you."

"I'd sooner hear it from you." They made their way to the back room.

"You know everything I know and probably a whole lot more."

The topic was left as they practiced.

She returned home in time to help prepare supper. It would be nice to have biscuits made again by Reese, but she hadn't invited him to join them for the meal lest anyone think there was more to their acquaintance than there was. People like Lisa, Sylvie, Jimmy, her sisters, her parents and likely the entire population of Glory and most of those in the surrounding area.

They hadn't said anything about practicing again with Reese and she wouldn't be the one to say she wondered if he'd come. She and Eve were playing a duet for the show so after supper, they went over to the church. Josie came along and leaned against the piano, tapping her toes to the lively music Victoria and Eve had chosen.

Josie suddenly straightened and looked to the back. "Well, look who's joining us."

Victoria continued to play as she glanced to the door. Reese. He'd come. And why she should think it was to see her, she couldn't say. Except his gaze sought and found hers as he called a greeting.

"I know you girls have your parts down solid but I'm a little shaky on mine. You see, cows aren't all that fussy about what notes I sing."

He joined them at the front and stood behind Victoria. "Am I interrupting?"

"Not at all," Eve said. "And it's true, you can use the practice. Vicki, play the hymn."

"What hymn?"

Eve nudged her. "The one the four of us are singing, of course." She leaned closer to whisper. "What's wrong with you?"

"Nothing. I didn't follow your meaning is all."

She must not. Could not.

She couldn't say what she meant. Only that her heart thumped like she'd run all the way from the river. And her thoughts felt as scrambled as eggs thrown at a brick wall.

## CHAPTER 5

The next day dragged on leaden feet as Reese tried his best to keep his hands and mind occupied with work. By midafternoon, he had done everything Mickey had for him to do.

"Run along and amuse yourself," the man said. "Maybe go visit that Kinsley gal Sylvie says you're interested in."

Reese held back a sigh. He'd not spent much time in a small town before, and the way everyone poked their noses into each other's business both annoyed and amused him. On one hand, it was good to know that they looked out for each other and that Victoria was protected by the whole town. But it might also be nice to go walking with a girl without everyone discussing it and deciding what it meant. In the end, he simply accepted it as being what it was. "Think I'll go for a ride and have a look at the country."

"Suit yourself. The country's nice, but nothing compared to that pretty little gal."

Reese wasn't about to argue, but he knew Victoria and the others would be busy preparing for the evening. Likely making fried chicken and cake for their box lunch. Besides, he had no good reason for hanging about.

He saddled Thunder. "You've been brushed until you shine. Good for Jimmy." They rode out of town to the east then turned north. Some of the land he rode through would border his ranch and he wanted to get a feel for the lay of it and any neighbors. He liked what he saw. "Thunder, we are going to have us a home where we can live and—" *Love.* He stopped before the word that sprang to his mind could come from his mouth. "I don't foresee love for me." But try as he would, he could not keep from picturing Victoria. Sure, she was pretty and talented and nice. But if he ever fell in love, he wanted it to be with someone who would offer him forever.

How could he expect that with someone who could be snatched away by her father any day? Or forget him if her memory ever returned? No, life with her would be full of uncertainty.

He glanced at the sky. Time to get back to town though he'd been slowly making his way that direction for the last few minutes. He took Thunder to the livery barn and cared for him. Then he made his way to the river, found a secluded spot, and had a cold bath.

Mickey had let him move into a room in the loft of the barn, and he went there to don his almost-new clothes and brush his hair into submission.

"You ready?" Mickey called. "We could walk over together."

"I'm coming." He hurried down the narrow stairs and gaped at his boss. The man he was used to seeing was tall and rangy, with a wild mop of dark blond hair. He was usually dressed in bib-front overalls that looked like they were made for a much larger person. This man had brushed his hair back and tied it with a length of leather. To Reese's surprise the color of Mickey's hair was several shades paler than he thought. He had shaved off the stubble he usually had on his face except for a neat moustache. And his clothes were so new they had crisp creases from being folded.

"Nice shirt," Reese said. It was red and white striped.

"Yup. Got new trousers too."

"You look mighty fine, Mickey." He clapped the man on the back.

Mickey grinned widely then shook his head. "Ain't nobody going to look at me when I come in with you at my side." He looked Reese up and down. "'Course it will be the young ones like Miss Victoria who will be looking at you. It will be older women who might give me a second glance. I'm the age for widows and spinsters."

Side by side they made their way to the church.

Reese wondered if Mickey had a special widow or spinster in mind. The evening looked about to turn even more interesting than Reese originally thought.

They reached the church where the talent show was going to be held. Tables and chairs had been set out in the yard for the meal and bits of gingham hung from the trees.

"Loves real festive," Mickey said.

They went into the church. Eve tended a table where she took the admission fee and for twenty-five cents registered those who were taking part in the show. Reese paid his fee then he and Mickey found a seat about halfway up the aisle.

Victoria played the piano as people entered. She watched those arriving and smiled at Reese. Of course, she smiled at everyone. No need for him to think she favored him above the others.

Not that he expected it. Or wanted it. No sir. His heart was sealed secure. The lock named Betty. The key that turned the lock keeping the door closed was named Trust. He'd vowed trust would not be squandered again.

That left Victoria barred from his heart. Simply put, she was pretty and appealing, but not someone to trust. He didn't know if she was a Hayworth or a lookalike. He didn't know why she was here or if she knew more than she admitted. He recalled her reaction to saying she had amnesia and, although he found it hard to confess, he wondered if she was an accomplished actress.

Certainly not someone whom he trusted enough to hand the key to his locked heart to.

The church was soon full with men standing at the back and others crowding to the windows to be able to hear.

The preacher went to the front. "Welcome to you all. It seems strange for me to stand here and not have a sermon prepared. But wait, who says I don't? After all, it's a talent show, and I like to think preaching is one of my talents."

A disgruntled murmur swept across the audience.

The preacher laughed. "Don't worry. No sermon today."

Reese chuckled and met Victoria's gaze. She shook

her head slightly as if to say her pa was trying to be funny and had failed.

Mr. Kinsley continued. "As you probably all know, this event is meant to raise funds to build a school for the town. We've done a number of things in the past and you've all faithfully attended, taken part, and contributed your money. We—my daughter, Victoria, especially—are hoping this event will bring the funds to the place we can order the materials and get the building up. I'm sure you all agree this is important for our town."

Everyone clapped.

"Now let's get started. While I bent your ear Josie and Eve have put all the entries together and created a program." Eve hurried up the aisle and handed her pa a sheet of paper. "First, is my four daughters singing a song they have composed together."

Lots of clapping and cheering as the four girls stood up. Victoria hummed a note and, without the accompaniment of the piano, they began a slow, haunting melody about love lost. Then suddenly the tempo changed, and the words indicated that the lost love had been found.

Reese wondered how much of the lyrics had been Victoria's. But wouldn't her worries be the opposite? Finding love and then losing it.

Several men recited poems as did two ladies who spoke with such fervor, Reese noticed several of the women in the audience wiping their eyes.

Victoria and Eve played their piano duet.

Then the preacher announced, "We have another quartet—Eve, Josie, Victoria and a newcomer, Reese Cartwright." He shook the sheet of paper. "I can't wait to hear this one."

Many laughed as he sat down.

Reese joined the others at the piano bench. Eve sat beside Victoria. Josie and Reese stood at their side, facing the audience. His voice cracked on the first note then Victoria smiled at him and he sang as they had practiced.

The song was over and, amidst clapping and whistles, he took his place by Mickey. "Didn't know you could sing," the man murmured.

"It's mostly cows that hear me." Victoria and Lisa slipped out the back. He supposed they were preparing for their entry.

After an elderly lady read a drab little story that Reese suspected she had written herself, Mr. Kinsley announced Victoria and Lisa.

They came in, dressed as old ladies. They sat on chairs and pretended to be rocking. It seemed they sat on the front porch of a house and observed the comings and goings of the townspeople. Both were hard of hearing, resulting in many hilarious misunderstandings.

When they finished, Reese clapped so hard his palms stung.

He already knew that Victoria had a keen sense of humor. It was one of the things he liked about her.

Before he could analyse that thought, the preacher announced, "Our final entry is Jimmy and his dog, Spot."

The audience grew quiet as Jimmy led Spot to the front. There were several murmurs. Likely a few protesting the dog's presence but no one spoke out as the preacher stood up front, his expression stern. Reese guessed everyone understood they were to treat this boy with kindness.

"My dog is right smart, ya know? Why, he's smarter than lots of people."

Reese chuckled along with many others. The boy probably had a good point.

"Spot can count and all sorts of stuff, but I know you won't believe me if I don't show you." He proceeded to prove his point by asking the dog many questions such as how many marbles did he have in his hand? He pretended to shoot the dog with his finger and Spot fell down dead so suddenly that Reese laughed. The dog saluted, shook his head for no, and put his front paws on the chair and bowed his head to pray.

"Was that fun?" Jimmy asked the dog. Spot grinned and nodded his head. The crowd erupted in laughter and clapping. Jimmy and Spot were the stars of the evening.

On his way down the aisle, Jimmy whispered in Reese's ear. "It's the one with the big red bow and a ruffle around the top."

"Excellent job, Jimmy and Spot," the preacher said. "Now if we move out to the side yard, I think there is an array of box lunches waiting to be consumed. Of course, the men have to buy them first."

As the crowd left the church, Reese waited for Victoria and fell in at her side. "A very enjoyable evening. Congratulations."

"Thanks. It was fun."

They gathered round the table holding the lunches.

Jimmy made his way through the crowd to Reese, his dog on one side and a worried-looking woman at the other.

"Mr. Reese, this is my ma. Mrs. Anderson."

Reese nodded. "Pleased to meet you, ma'am. Your boy

is a great help."

Jimmy grinned at the praise. "Did you like what my dog did?"

"It was very entertaining. You must have spent a lot of time teaching him all those tricks."

Mrs. Anderson chuckled. "They are never apart."

Victoria and Mrs. Anderson exchanged greetings then the preacher called for their attention. "I'm happy to turn the auction over to Mickey."

Reese leaned over to speak softly to Victoria. "The man is full of surprises." He studied the box lunches on the table. Red bow and ruffles? Several had red bows.

Jimmy nudged him and tipped his head to the right.

Reese followed the boy's direction and spotted a basket with a red bow and a ruffle just as Jimmy had said. He leaned back, prepared to wait until it was offered.

Mickey lifted a basket wrapped in a dish towel. He sniffed. "This smells delicious and has a good weight to it. Whoever buys this one will enjoy a good meal. What am I bid?"

The bidding was brisk with Mickey's comments urging them on.

One after another, the baskets were claimed by the buyers. The preacher had said in order to keep it fair, the owner of the basket mustn't reveal herself until the baskets were all sold and the buyers had paid for them.

Then a basket in a snow-white cloth was held up.

Beside him, Jimmy quivered and Reese knew this one belonged to his mother.

"What am I bid?" Mickey asked.

"Ten cents." Jimmy called.

"Ten cents it is." Mickey looked across the crowd. "I

A LOVE TO CHERISH

have a bid for fifteen cents. Do I hear one for twenty? Twenty? Well, then—"

"Sixteen," Jimmy called.

"Sixteen. Do I hear—I have a bid for twenty cents."

Reese glanced to his right and left. He could not see anyone bidding but Mickey was far too kind a man to run Jimmy's bid up.

"Twenty-one," Jimmy called.

"I have a bid for twenty-five."

Jimmy pulled the coins out of his pocket and counted them.

His ma leaned over. "Save your money. Let someone else buy the lunch."

Jimmy curled his fist about the coins. "Twenty-seven cents."

Mickey looked at Jimmy with an expression of regret. "Son, I have a bid for two dollars. Can you beat that?"

The crowd gasped at the price offered.

Jimmy shook his head.

"Then I claim the basket." Another gasp and some titters at his announcement.

Jimmy looked surprised and then angry.

Reese figured the only thing stopping him from erupting was his mother's hand on his shoulder and her soft words. "It's all for a good cause."

Then the basket with the red bow and ruffles was lifted.

"A very pretty basket," Mickey said. "What am I bid?"

Reese waited, wanting to know what he would face for competition.

"Twenty-five cents." Reese recognized Arnie from the previous Sunday.

"Thirty." That was Teller, another cowboy from Sunday dinner.

"Thirty-five." Reese didn't recognize the bidder but he was another cowboy who likely had been at one of the Kinsley's Sunday dinners.

Arnie, Teller, and the third cowboy bid back and forth.

"Forty. Forty-five. Fifty."

The third cowboy dropped out.

"Fifty-five. Fifty-six." The pair hesitated longer with each bit.

Reese guessed they would soon drop out too.

The pause between bids lengthened until Mickey was about to call, "Sold."

"Five dollars," Reese said, and a hush fell over the crowd.

Beside him, Victoria gasped.

"Sold," Mickey called.

From behind him somewhere, someone called, "That'a boy, Reese." He recognized Sylvie's voice.

The crowd laughed and clapped.

"Reese," Victoria whispered. "What are you doing?"

"Buying a lunch in a pretty basket." It pleased him to see her cheeks had become as rosy as a summer sunrise. "It's for a good cause." He leaned back, satisfied with the way things were going.

Soon after that the auction ended. Reese lined up to pay his money and then he claimed the basket.

He backed away from the table where Mr. Kinsley took the money and waited for Victoria though he was wise enough to pretend he looked about as if wondering who he would eat with.

\* \* \*

VICTORIA STAYED with her sisters even after Reese moved aside, holding her basket and looking around expectantly.

Eve gave her a questioning look. "Shouldn't you join him? After all, he paid well to share your lunch." She waggled her eyebrows.

"I'm going." She took three steps in his direction.

Sylvie watched, waiting to see whose lunch Reese had purchased. She saw Victoria and plowed toward her. "I knew he had his eyes on you. You just be careful. Just because he's young and handsome don't mean he's kind and honorable." She joined Teller, who had bought her basket. She might not be his first choice of companion, but he wouldn't regret the meal she'd prepared.

Victoria's footsteps faltered as Sylvie departed. Did the woman know something about Reese that Victoria didn't? Not that there was any way she could avoid him. She was obligated to share her basket of food.

There were blankets available for those who preferred to eat picnic style, and Reese scooped one up and led them to an open spot. They were close to Jimmy, his ma, and Mickey. Victoria wondered if that was intentional. She'd seen the way Reese had looked at Jimmy when Mickey outbid him and guessed Reese might be concerned how the boy would handle it.

They couldn't help but overhear the conversation of the three nearby. Jimmy's ma opened the lunch. Victoria's father had asked a blessing upon the food, so no one had to wait to start.

Mickey looked into the basket. "This looks yummy.

Before we start, I want to get something clear. Jimmy, I outbid you for two reasons. First, to let you save your money, and also because I wanted a chance to talk to you and your ma."

"What you want?" Jimmy's frown had turned to curiosity.

Victoria leaned close to whisper to Reese. "I've never known that boy to stay angry more than a minute. He's too good-natured to hang on to grudges."

"He's a good boy."

The both listened without appearing to do so.

Mickey continued. "Jimmy, I've seen how you work. I could use a young fella like you." He held up his hands to stop either Jimmy or his ma from saying anything. "Let me finish. I know we will soon have a school, and I'm all for book learnin'. So what I'm offering is for you to work a few hours after school. So long as it doesn't interfere with your studies. Mrs. Anderson, what do you think of that?"

"I think that's a very kind offer and please, would you call me Martha?"

"I'd be pleased to, and it's necessity that makes me want to hire the boy. Reese is going to his ranch any day now and I could use the help."

"Ma, can I? Please."

The boy was so excited, Victoria thought he would jump right out of his boots, if he wore any.

"Yes, you may. Tell Mr. Mickey thank you."

"Thank you and I will work really hard."

"I know you will. Now let's eat."

Victoria thought perhaps she should let Reese eat too

and opened her basket. But something troubled her. "Did you know this was my lunch?"

He widened his eyes. "How would I know that?" He looked into the basket. "Fried chicken. Good, I hoped for that. Bean salad. You know I haven't had this since my ma served it to me. And chocolate cake. Shall we?" He offered chicken to Victoria.

She was not about to be deterred. "My sisters might have told you."

"I assure you they didn't." He bit into the chicken. "Very tasty and tender."

She saw him wink at Jimmy. Jimmy grinned widely.

"It was you, Jimmy Anderson." She tried to sound scolding but wondered how successful she'd been.

Jimmy managed to look so innocent she laughed and turned back to Reese. "Why would you pay that much for a box lunch?"

"Isn't it obvious?"

"Not to me."

"It's for a good cause."

"Thank you." The answer did not satisfy. What was she wanting to hear? That he wanted to share her lunch? Did she think he was letting everyone know that he meant to court her?

A bit of distance away, her gaze met Lisa's. Lisa nodded and smiled.

Victoria looked away. She'd fulfilled her promise to Lisa by accepting Reese's invitation to walk her home. She'd spent time with him practicing for the talent show. But as Mickey said, he would soon be going to his ranch. Her life wasn't such she could hope for anything but friendship with him. She should be relieved he was leaving.

She wasn't.

"I'm glad to help get a school in this town, but there might be another reason I bid high." A beat of waiting.

"And what would that be?"

"I wanted to make sure I got your basket."

She couldn't break from his intent look, his gaze so steady, so dark, so compelling. "Why?" She blurted out the word before she realized it sounded like she wanted more. And she did.

"So I could enjoy your company."

She ducked her head. Heat rushed to her cheeks. Why did he care? She slowly brought her head up. "You know I am a woman with no memory of my past."

"So you said."

"Seems that makes my future somewhat shaky too."

"Depends what you're wanting in the future. I know what I want."

"You're going leave for your ranch soon." Her insides ached though she told herself that couldn't be.

"Abe is expecting me."

"Do you have a young woman in mind to share your new life? Someone from Chicago perhaps?"

He ate a mouthful of the bean salad. "This is as good as Ma used to make."

"Thanks." Seems he didn't mean to answer.

He finished his bean salad then sighed. "I had a girl I thought loved me. Betty. Turns out she only wanted to prove to her friends that she could make me fall in love with her." He set aside his plate with jerky movements. "In my mind, love should be open and honest. It should be real and forever. Not pretend. Not simply convenient. Not easily forgotten."

His words should encourage her. Give her hope. But instead, they sucked hope right out of her and left her as discouraged as she could possibly be. She could never be sure of forever. And how could she be open and honest when she didn't know what her past held?

"I'm sorry you had such an experience. I look at Ma and Pa and think that is what love should look like. They've been married thirty years. They've dealt with many disappointments and challenges. They are always there for each other."

"Look at Jimmy's ma. She's widowed. Do you think she'll remarry?"

She watched the woman with Mickey, wondering why Reese had changed the subject. A touch of pink stained Martha's cheeks. "I suppose it would make sense. It would give Jimmy a pa and ease the burden she carries in supporting them."

"My ma remarried four months after Pa died."

Victoria tried to hide her surprise.

Reese continued. "When she told me what she planned to do I said it was too soon. I asked how she could forget Pa so quickly. She said she didn't expect me to understand. I said I understood well enough. 'Love,' I said, 'is just pretend. A way to get someone to pay the bills.' I regret saying that. Ma didn't deserve it. Life had been hard with Pa though he was a good man when he wasn't drinking. Trouble was he got to drinking more and more frequently. Ralph was kind to her while I was at home. I hope it continued."

Victoria handed him a large portion of cake.

He stared at it.

"Is something wrong?"

"No." He took a bite. "It's good. I was only thinking how hard it is to tell what's real when it comes to love." A pause and then he added, "And other things."

His words felt like an accusation. But how could she defend herself? She wasn't pretending, but neither was she real.

"My whole life is based on a non-existent foundation. I can't be real, because I don't know who I am." She scrambled to her feet, looking for Ma. The one place she felt safe was in Ma's presence.

Reese caught her hand. "Don't run away. I wasn't meaning you. I was only thinking how thoroughly Betty fooled me. I gave my heart to her only to learn she didn't want it."

She didn't pull away from his grasp. Rather, she squeezed his hand. "It's a hard lesson to learn." She sat down again and nibbled at a piece of cake. "I think your ma maybe hurt you as much as Betty did, only in a slightly different way." Her heart ached to think of the boy Reese being so disillusioned by his mother's choice and then being deceived by a young woman.

She glanced at Martha and silently prayed the woman would be sure any friendship with Mickey was good for Jimmy.

Reese leaned closer. "I apologize."

She jerked around to face him. "For what?" He looked so worried she lifted her hand, intending to wipe away the frown lines around his eyes. Realizing how that could be misinterpreted by those watching and even by Reese, she dropped her hand to her lap.

"This was supposed to be a fun evening and I've turned it into a funeral dirge."

She laughed at his mournful tone. "You can change it back into dancing."

"Okay." He chuckled. "Are you by any chance thinking of the same thing I am?"

"I don't know. What are you thinking?"

"That we sound like a Bible verse."

The grin that turned her lips up came from a sweet spot deep in her heart. "'I will turn their mourning into joy, and will comfort them, and make them rejoice from their sorrow.'"

"Good one, but I was thinking of, 'We have piped unto you, and ye have not danced; we have mourned unto you, and ye have not lamented.'"

They held each other's gazes as they chuckled.

Victoria blinked first. "I'm a preacher's daughter, so it's expected that I know lots of Scriptures. But how is it you seem to?"

"You mean me being a cowboy and all."

"I haven't forgotten you're a cowboy who sings to your cows."

His eyes darkened, inviting her into their depths.

She resisted. She could not be what he wanted. Nor could he give her what she wanted—her past. She shuddered.

"Are you okay?" He glanced about. "Did you see someone who alarmed you?"

"I'm fine." But the idea of getting her past at the cost of losing her present hollowed her insides to an echoing abandoned building. "You were going to tell me about how you know so many verses."

"Did I say that?"

"If you didn't, I'm sure you meant to."

They grinned at each other.

"It's a very mundane story."

"I might enjoy hearing it anyway." She knew she stared at him far too long and if anyone watched, they would be coming to the wrong conclusion. Aware that Sylvie would be nearby, Victoria lowered her gaze to the now empty plate that had once held a piece of cake. When had she eaten it?

"If you're sure you won't be bored…"

"I'm very sure."

"Okay. Like I said, there's nothing very glamorous about it."

She gave him a stern look. "Reese, are you stalling?"

He laughed softly. "Maybe. It's fun to tease you."

She tried her best to frown at him but ended up laughing. One thing she liked about this man was how he amused her. "Too many people take themselves and life too seriously." She held up her hand before he could protest. "Not that life isn't a serious matter. But it doesn't have to be a funeral dirge."

"I agree. Now do you want to hear my story, or not?"

"Oh yes, please." She batted her eyes and looked as beguiling as she knew how to.

"Don't do that." He gave a furtive look around. "If your pa sees he will come over here and box my ears."

She laughed so hard she was sure half the crowd looked her way. Not wanting to give people the wrong impression, she ducked her head and pressed her lips together.

"That's better," he whispered. He cleared his throat

and began to speak at a normal volume. "Two years ago I was wintering on a ranch. Me and an old guy by the name of Hoot—"

"Hoot? You're surely joshing."

"Nope. It's what he told me. We were the only ones staying in the bunkhouse. It was a nasty winter. Lots of snow. Lots of days we couldn't go anywhere but to the cookhouse and back. Long, boring days." He dragged out the words to indicate what he meant and yawned. "I looked at Hoot and said, 'We are going to perish of boredom before spring.' Hoot hooted—don't laugh. He said, 'I got ways of passing winter days.'

"'Yeah? Don't mind if you tell me,' I said, thinking he liked to play cards or whittle. Nope. He goes to his saddle bag and takes out a little black book. It was a tiny Bible. Smallest thing I ever saw. He used a magnifying glass to read it." Reese shook his head as if still surprised by that fact.

"You gonna read the winter away?" I said.

"He said we could, but he had something a little more challenging in mind."

"He went on to explain that we could take turns finding a verse in the Bible and challenge ourselves to memorize it. The one who got it word perfect first was the winner. Didn't sound like much fun to me and I said so. Well, he said we could make it a little more interesting.

"He had my attention so of course I asked how. Forfeits, he said. We were each to give up something or do something for the other person if we lost. Well, I knew he had a stash of hard candy and I sure did crave that, so I agreed, thinking it would be easy to memorize stuff faster than an old man. I soon discovered it was hard. We took turns choosing verses. I picked the hardest ones I could find. He beat me time and again. I ended up giving up my spare pair of socks, a little knife I had bought in Texas, a hair ribbon of Betty's. Don't ask why I kept that. Then he made me go outside to do the chores on my own. He made me go ask the cook for extra cookies. Made me brew coffee over the fire. Then I got serious. I picked easy verses. I maybe cheated a little and picked them before I told him so I could work on them ahead of time. And I started to win. I got my socks and knife back. I got some of his hard candies. He made the coffee." Reese chuckled. "Could be he let me win to give me some incentive."

"Hoot sounds like a wise old fellow. You sure his name was Hoot and you aren't making it up."

"Hoot is what he told me, and I had no reason to question him about it."

She leaned closer and squinted at him. "Did you say you cheated?"

He grinned. "I said I might have. And I'm not saying anything more."

She was about to point out the irony of learning Bible verses while cheating when Pa called for attention.

"You'll all want to know how much money we raised?"

Victoria bit her bottom lip. Would they have enough to build the school? Would they allow her to teach? She didn't have any proof of her education, but she knew history, English, some sciences, mathematics, and so many other things. She knew she'd had a good education.

Why could she remember that and not who she was?

# CHAPTER 6

Reese watched Victoria worry her bottom lip as she waited for her father to announce how successful the evening had been. In Reese's opinion it had been very successful. He'd enjoyed the entertainment both at the talent show and from Victoria at his side. There was only one dark spot in the evening and that was his own stupidity. Why had he not-so-subtly warned her that he would settle for nothing less than honesty? That wasn't quite what he meant. Authenticity. That was it. Something real that would allow him to use that trust key and open his heart.

He wasn't warning her. He was warning himself. He needed to keep reminding himself. No doubt she was being as honest as she could be. But amnesia—or some other reason aside—he was almost convinced she was Constance Hayworth, not Victoria Kinsley. He'd know for certain once he heard back from his ma.

And if she was? Sooner or later that truth would be forced upon her.

He realized Mr. Kinsley was talking.

"So, it is with joy and gratitude toward you good folk and to our heavenly Father who supplies all our needs that I announce that we have enough money to order the material for the school."

The audience clapped and cheered. Everyone was getting to their feet. Reese stood and helped Victoria up.

"Congratulations. Your hard work has paid off." Mickey patted her on the back.

One by one, the majority of the town's people filed by congratulating Victoria.

Then there was a flurry of activity as people gathered up their belongings and their children and left.

Her family gathered around them, pressing Reese into their midst.

Several times, Reese tried to excuse himself, but each time one of the Kinsleys stood in the way of his departure and he was helplessly shepherded home with them.

"I should go," he protested.

"Doesn't look like they want you to," Kade said. "Best to simply go along with it." He patted Reese on the back. "You'll get used to them."

Reese shrugged. He didn't mind at the moment but wasn't sure he should allow himself to be treated like one of the family. Nevertheless, he joined them as they crowded around the table to go over the evening, telling and retelling the best parts.

Stella didn't stay up long. She escorted the children to bed. Victoria had told him how Kade and Flora had discovered her near death and brought her to the manse. The evening had worn out the poor woman.

Eve made tea. Josie served them more cake. And Victoria bubbled with excitement.

"We'll soon have a school. I can't wait. Pa, have you talked to the others about letting me teach?"

"The board is in agreement with you taking the job."

Victoria grabbed Eve's hands and swung her around the room. "Finally, I will have something useful to do."

Eve ground to a halt, pulling Victoria's gleeful dance to an end. "Isn't cooking, baking, and taking care of others useful?" Eve sounded offended.

A glance around the table and Reese thought all the women seemed to feel the comment somehow belittled their work.

"Of course, it's useful," Victoria said. "But I have all this knowledge inside my head. I might as well share it with others." Her exuberance died and she sat down in the chair next to Reese.

He could feel her quivering and wanted to offer comfort by way of a touch but wasn't at ease doing it in front of the others.

She sniffled. "Why is it I can remember all sorts of stuff that's only good for teaching, but I can't remember my own name?" She looked about the table, her cheeks wet with tears. "I can't remember what truly matters."

Reese clenched his fists beneath the table. If someone didn't reach out to her soon, and soothe away her tears, he would do it, in front of family or not.

Mrs. Kinsley pushed her chair back and rushed to Victoria's side. "Oh, sweet child. I wish you could remember all the things you want to. I would give you up to your past if it made you happy. But unless that happens, you are as much our daughter as you possibly could be. Everything you do is of value. Not only to us and those around us but to our heavenly Father."

The girls all crowded to her side. The preacher stood behind her and cupped his hand to her head. "Child, you are loved."

Reese swallowed back a lump the size of a small boulder.

Victoria pulled a handkerchief from her pocket and dried her eyes. "I'm sorry. I don't know what's come over me lately. I know I won't likely get my past back and that's all right. I'm happy right here." She gave them each a teary smile.

Reese realized she was, as she said, happy here. But would she ever get over longing for her past?

When would he hear from Ma? With train service the mail came and went regularly. Perhaps in a week he'd hear back. If she said Constance Hayworth was safe in the bosom of her family then Reese could accept Victoria was an unfortunate victim of the train accident. If Ma said the girl was still missing? Wouldn't he be honor bound to contact Mr. Hayworth? If he did, he knew what would happen. The man would snatch her from this loving family, the only family she could remember.

Before he decided what to do, he had to make sure it would do more good than harm. But he wasn't sure how he could know that.

In all fairness he needed to let the preacher know of his suspicions even before he heard back from Ma. He would speak privately to the preacher the first chance he got and tell him what he suspected. Somehow the truth would be revealed.

. . .

THE NEXT DAY he rode out to see Abe Shaw. Abe had not begun to pack his belongings.

"It's harder than I realized to say goodbye to everything that I shared with my family. I just wish I could forget it all."

"Is forgetting the best thing?" He thought of Victoria. Was it best for her to not know who she was before her accident?

"I need to move forward but I can't so long as I cling to the past." The man looked about the room, no doubt seeing his wife and children in every object and every inch.

"Take your time about moving. I have a temporary job at the livery barn." Though Mikey would be wanting Jimmy to start.

"Thank you. I appreciate that. But treat the place like it's yours."

"I'll ride out and check the cows. Do you want to come with me?"

"Sure do." The man was obviously happy to not have to deal with the contents of the house.

They rode the perimeter of the land that would be Reese's as soon as the final papers were signed, but in both his mind and Abe's it was his already. It was a fine sunny day. He enjoyed the ride and the visit, but he missed town. Or maybe, he missed certain people who lived there.

They returned to the house late in the day.

"You'll join me for supper, won't you?" Abe asked.

Reese thought of refusing but sensed the man needed company. "Sounds like a fine idea. I'll make biscuits."

Abe blinked and then chuckled. "Not often you hear of a cowboy who bakes."

"I don't do much, but I found learning a few skills is preferable to existing on beans and canned peaches."

"Sounds a lot like my diet of late. But I think the occasion calls for a bottle of my wife's canned meat."

"You have any potatoes and carrots, maybe a turnip, to throw in with the meat?"

Abe seemed surprised that making a stew was that easy. "I believe I do."

The pair soon had the vegetables and meat cooking together and Reese slid a tray of biscuits into the hot oven. He'd made a big batch knowing Abe would enjoy them for another day or two.

"Have you decided what you're going to do when you leave here?" Reese asked.

"Still haven't made up my mind. This here"—he indicated the house—"was our dream." He shrugged. "Can't seem to think of something else I want to do. Maybe head to California and look for gold." He slumped forward. "Can't seem to drum up enthusiasm for the task."

"Maybe you should work for a rancher until you know what you want."

"Maybe." There was no enthusiasm in the man's response.

"Have you thought of packing your saddle bags and simply riding into the mountains until you feel ready to do something else?"

Abe sat up. "That's a good idea. But what do I do with all this stuff?" He waved his hand around the room.

"Do you want to sell some of it? If you do, I could use

it. The rest you could crate up and store on the place until you need it."

Abe smacked his hands together. "I like that idea. Give me a few days to sort things out."

"I'll give you a fair price for whatever you want to part with."

"Let's talk again next week, if that's all right with you. I hope you don't mind the delay."

"Next week is fine. I'm satisfied that things are in fine shape here. No need for you to rush away."

By the time he headed back to town, the sun dipped toward the mountains. He sidetracked past the church and manse out of curiosity. The church was dark. Lamplight glowed from the kitchen window in the manse. He paused to study the square of light. It was too late for a social call and he had no other excuse for going to the door, so he turned Thunder toward the livery barn.

Mickey sat on a chair outside the barn. Jimmy sat cross-legged on the ground beside the chair.

"Wondered if you'd get back before dark," Mickey said.

"I'll be around a few more days, if that's all right with you."

"Fine by me. Jimmy is going to start coming by morning and evening. If I'm not around, you could maybe show him what needs to be done."

Jimmy bolted to his feet. "I can brush the horses. Sweep the floors. Clean out the stalls. Put out feed." The boy sounded so eager, Reese decided he wouldn't be doing much for fear of getting in the way of what Jimmy planned to do.

"You can do about anything you set your mind to," Mickey said, and squeezed Jimmy's shoulder.

The boy glowed with enjoyment of Mickey's approval.

Reese knew Mickey would treat the boy right, whether simply as an employer or as a stepfather.

"You get on home now before your ma starts to worry." Mickey turned Jimmy toward home and the boy raced away.

"I won't be keeping Jimmy from what you have in mind for him." Reese unsaddled his horse and tended him as they talked.

"I don't expect him to work like a man. Just a boy doing his best to help his ma." Mickey unwound from the wall and went to his room.

Reese went to his. He'd give Abe a few days to sort of his belongings. After that Reese would have no reason to remain in town.

Not that he wanted one. Or so he told himself.

SUNDAY MORNING he rose early and prepared for the church service. It had been a long time since he'd seen Victoria and was anxious for a glimpse of her. And a conversation.

He scolded himself. It was Friday night he'd seen her. Not a long time, he reasoned.

But it felt like weeks.

Mickey had left by the time Reese was ready. He wasn't surprised to see him walking down the street with Jimmy and Jimmy's widowed ma beside him.

Reese reached the church. He stepped into the cool

interior. Victoria played the piano, saw him and smiled. Yes, she smiled at all those who entered but not as warmly as she smiled at him.

He resisted an urge to press the heel of his hand to his forehead. Perhaps he should ride out to his ranch earlier than he'd agreed to. Before his brain turned to mush, because it was already showing signs of doing so.

Redheaded Flora and her husband, Kade, sat beside Eve and Josie. Mrs. Kinsley sat at the far end of the pew. There wasn't room for Reese even if he'd thought to sit there, which he hadn't. He slipped into a pew partway forward.

His gaze went toward Victoria. She mouthed something. It took him a moment to realize she was saying "cows." He grinned at the reminder that he mostly sang for cows.

After the service, Mrs. Kinsley spoke to him. "You'll join us for dinner, won't you?"

"I'd love to." He followed the family from the church. Almost stumbled when he saw that one of the other cowboys going the same direction was Smitty.

Reese dropped back so he walked in step with the man. "What are you doing here?"

"Same as you. Planning to enjoy a free meal." Smitty slowed so the two of them were alone. "Or do you have something else in yer mind?"

Truth was, Reese did. He'd hoped to talk to Victoria. Maybe ask for her to walk to the river with him. "Nope."

"Is she the gal?" Smitty tipped his head to indicate who he meant though it was clear in Reese's mind. He tried to think what he could say to divert Smitty from pursuing the matter.

"Did you get the job?" he asked.

"I ain't here to talk about work." Smitty lengthened his steps so they caught up to the others.

Reese had no intention of carrying on the conversation in the Kinsleys' hearing. But he gritted his teeth as he tried to think of a way to dissuade Smitty from his interest. He gritted them even more when Smitty managed to sit next to Victoria at the meal.

The preacher asked Smitty to introduce himself.

"I just go by Smitty. Can't rightly recall if I have any other name." He managed to look both sad and confused. "Grew up alone apart from a few years in an orphanage. Been on my own since I was a tadpole. Did whatever I had to in order to survive."

Of course, the story garnered murmurs of sympathy, but Reese wondered how much was true, especially when Smitty gave him a triumphant look. Reese guessed the man meant to inform him that he knew how to get on the good side of these people.

"That's sad," Victoria said.

"Sounds like a tough way to grow up," Eve said.

Reese wondered if he heard a hesitation in her voice.

Flora gave the man hard study. "We're all orphaned, us Kinsleys. So we kind of know what you're talking about."

If there was any way Reese could warn the Kinsleys not to believe everything Smitty said, he would do it. He glanced at the preacher in time to see him exchange a look with his wife.

Reese grinned. Maybe the man wasn't prepared to fall hook, line, and sinker for the story.

Reese forced his jaw to relax. He'd hang about as

much as he could, but the preacher was no fool. He'd surely discern fact from fiction.

But that knowledge troubled Reese. If Victoria was really Miss Hayworth, why hadn't the preacher searched out that fact? None of it made any sense. He was beginning to hope that everything that led him to believe she was the missing girl was only coincidence. But that was a lot of chance facts coming together.

Conversation around the table eventually turned to talk of the school. Smitty lost interest. He turned to Victoria. "I'd 'preciate it, if you'd show me 'round the town."

Her hesitation was plain to all. She glanced toward her pa, a helpless look on her face.

Reese pushed back. "I'll be glad to show you around." He waited for Smitty to get to his feet, his face dark with displeasure.

"On second thought, I better get back to the ranch 'fore I lose my job." He smiled at Mrs. Kinsley. "Thank you for the grand meal."

Reese sank back to his chair as the preacher walked the man to the door then returned and took his seat again.

For a moment, no one spoke. Flora burst out in laughter. "Do I sense some rivalry?"

Reese kept his expression blank. Let them think whatever they wanted. They did not know the danger Smitty posed. He was about to ask to speak privately to the preacher when the man began to talk.

"Victoria, I know you're anxious to get on with plans for building the school. We all are. But I can't do it at the moment."

"Pa, why not?"

"You remember Stewart Kennedy, the man who lives up in the hills?" He went on without waiting for an answer. "I got a message this morning from his neighbor. Stewart has had a bad fall. His leg is broken. He needs care. He asked that I come. I've discussed it with your mother, and she agrees I should go and see what the man needs. I understand he refuses to be moved to town, so I will stay with him as long as I'm needed. I'll return for Sunday service, of course."

Victoria blinked. "Of course, you must do what you need to do."

"Sir, if I may," Reese said, bringing all eyes to him. "I could go look after this Mr. Kennedy."

The preacher looked to his wife and some sort of communication passed silently between them.

"Reese," the preacher said, "that is a very kind offer, and in most cases I would gladly accept, but Stewart is a strange customer. Crusty and ready to believe the worst of people. I fear if I sent you instead of going myself, he will interpret it to mean I don't feel he is worth my time. I can't do that."

Victoria smiled though Reese could tell it took an effort.

If only he could do something to ease her disappointment. Maybe he could.

"Then perhaps you'd let me look after the building project."

He couldn't miss the eager look in Victoria's face as she turned to her father.

The preacher studied Reese for a moment. "Have you done anything like this in the past?"

"I worked side by side with a man who built a house and then a barn. I can assure you I know how to measure and cut. Not to brag, but I know how to judge the amount of material a building needs."

Mr. Kinsley looked around the table. "Does anyone see a problem with me turning the project over to Reese?"

"No, Pa," several voices said.

"I will need to get approval from the board members. I don't like to conduct business on the Sabbath, but I need to get out to Stewart's place as soon as possible." He pushed back from the table. "Give me an hour or two to speak to the others and I'll let you know."

Reese stared after the departing man, then brought his gaze to Victoria's.

"That's very kind of you, especially considering you have your own affairs to take care of," she said.

"It's for a good cause." He hoped his voice didn't sound as grating to the others as it did to him.

She ducked her head but not before he caught a flash of something in her eyes that made him think she was disappointed with his answer.

Did she hope he had done it for her sake?

He couldn't deny he had. He didn't like to see her disappointed, and it would enable him to make sure Smitty didn't make a nuisance of himself.

It seemed too much to hope they wouldn't see more of the man.

\* \* \*

AT BEDTIME VICTORIA sat at the writing desk in front of the window trying to decide what to write in her journal. What she wrote was not private. Everyone knew she kept track of the events of her life. Knowing the pages were available for anyone to read, she couldn't put in things that were private.

That meant she couldn't write down that it appeared Reese had come to her rescue twice in the afternoon.

First, he'd spared her from having to walk Smitty about town. There was something about the man that set her nerves on edge. She couldn't say exactly what it was. Or it might simply be that he seemed rough compared to Reese.

Then Reese had offered to take over the building project from Pa.

She could write that down. *Pa returned a couple of hours later with the announcement that the board members were agreeable. Norm White offered to help with ordering materials. He's had a lot of experience doing that and it gave the board members some assurance the money would be spent wisely. Reese wanted more information about the school—dimensions and so forth. We have agreed to go to the building site tomorrow and discuss plans. Pa left as soon as he'd delivered the news. We might not see him until the end of the week. Lord, help him be patient with this man. May Pa be able to make him understand that Jesus loves him.*

She finished with writing how Flora had teased her about two men vying for a chance to take her walking.

Victoria blotted the page. She would not think about the risks of letting herself care about someone. She would think only of the school project.

. . .

THE NEXT MORNING was laundry day. She liked seeing the washed clothes flap on the line, then smelling their fresh cleanness when they were brought in. As soon as dinner was over, she asked Ma if she could go to the building site.

"Take Eve with you."

Eve grinned at her. "I'll try not to get in your way."

"Oh hush. We're only going to pace out the building and go over the list of supplies Pa started."

Laughing together they left the manse and made their way toward the place where the school would be built.

She saw Reese as they turned the corner at the end of the block. His hat was pushed back. He stood with his hands on his hips, his legs wide, and seemed to be studying something. Her breath caught.

Eve nudged her. "A self-assured man is a good-looking man."

Victoria dug deep for the strength to steady her voice. "Did you have someone particular in mind?" Look how innocent she sounded.

Eve chuckled. "I guess you'll have to figure that out yourself."

They were close enough to where Reese stood that Victoria didn't answer. He turned at the sound of their approach and smiled at them both. *Both*, she silently informed Eve.

"Did your pa get away?" he asked.

"He left before supper. Said Stewart might be getting hungry if no one had been to see him since Saturday afternoon."

"I feel privileged that he entrusted me with this task." Reese saw the papers Victoria had. "Are those the plans?"

"And some work Pa has done on them." She showed the drawing of the school as they envisioned it then the list of materials that Pa had started.

He bent his head close to hers as they looked it over.

He straightened. "It looks good on paper. Where will it be on this lot?"

"Pa said the board had put stakes where it is to be." They looked around. "There's one." She pointed.

"And the others. Two, three, four." They walked what would be the perimeter of the building. Eve trailed along, humming to herself.

They came back to the front, where the door would be.

"Did your pa have something in mind for the construction?"

"Not that I know of. Why?"

"Have you heard of a barn raising?"

She chuckled. "I've been to a couple."

"Why don't we have a school raising as soon as the lumber comes in? The building would go up in one afternoon that way."

"A community event. What a good idea. I don't want people to think this is a Kinsley project or mine."

Eve was at Victoria's elbow. "It was you who insisted we needed a school."

"I'm sure someone else would have suggested it if I hadn't. After all, there are lots of children in town."

Reese studied the drawing and walked back to study the layout. He turned to consider the whole yard.

She wondered what he was thinking.

He rolled the papers together. "Let's go talk to Mr. White."

The three of them trooped down the street toward the store. Before they got there, Jimmy and half a dozen children trailed after them along with several dogs.

"We heard ya were going to start the school," Jimmy said. "How long you suppose it will take to build it?"

Reese looked at the parade of children on their heels. "I feel like the Pied Piper," he murmured.

Victoria stared at him. "That's an odd tale for you to be familiar with."

"Me being a cowboy and all," he drawled.

"Let me guess. It's something Hoot told you."

He laughed. "The man had a good store of stories from literature."

He faced the gathering of children. "How many of you are anxious to go to school?"

Two little girls held up their hands.

"How many of you like good stories?" Most of the hands went up.

"Well, Jimmy here tells me Miss Victoria is a good storyteller. What was it you said she told you, Jimmy?"

The boy bristled with importance. "She told me how Montana Territory came to be part of America when some president bought a bunch of land from the French."

The children looked impressed.

Jimmy turned to Victoria. "You gonna be the teacher?"

"Yes, I am, and I hope to see every one of you in school. I promise you won't regret it."

"If she's gonna teach," Jimmy addressed the others, "school might not be so bad."

Laughing at Jimmy's faint praise, Victoria turned to Reese. "Are we going to talk to Norm?" She glanced around. Where had Eve gone? There she was. Standing to the side watching someone Victoria couldn't see. She wondered who it could be. She'd ask about it later if she remembered.

The children went on down the street and Victoria and Reese went into the store.

Eve followed a moment later.

"What were you looking at?" Victoria asked her.

"Martha. She carried a plate of something to the livery barn."

"That's nice."

They grinned at each other and then Victoria joined Reese at the counter where he unrolled the plans for Norm to look at.

An hour later, they emerged. Victoria could barely contain her excitement. "I've dreamed of this for a long time. Even before we came to Glory, I thought of teaching. When we got here, I saw the need. Now to think the school will soon be built." She would have done a little dance right there in the middle of the street. She wanted to grab Reese's hand and lift their arms to the sky and shout, but neither was proper behavior for a future schoolteacher. She walked on demurely.

Eve had left before the order was finished so she and Reese were alone. Unless she remembered that a person was never alone in a small town. Even the buildings seemed to have eyes and ears.

"I don't want to go home. I'm too excited." She glanced about, hoping no ears or walls had heard her boldness.

"Then may I suggest a walk along the river?"

"Yes, you may." They turned that direction. Victoria

knew it was excitement about the school that made the grass appear greener, the sky a shimmering blue, and the waters silvery.

"A week to get the material all here. A work bee, and then it will be up." She couldn't hold back a squeal.

He grinned at her. "I'll work with Norm to get everything ready for the school raising." Norm had suggested the Tuesday following the arrival of the lumber for the event.

As they walked along, she laughed for no apparent reason. "You must think I'm addled."

He stopped and faced her. "I think you are very excited."

"Yes, I am."

They stopped by some trees. "Shall we sit and enjoy nature?"

"I'd like that." They sank to the soft grass overlooking the river. The air about them was filled with a wild aroma of poplar trees, hidden flowers, and the moist scent of the water rippling by. She sighed.

"I have always loved books. I like the feel of them. The smell of them. I like the worlds they invite me into. Even though I can't remember my past, I know I loved books even then. I know I was surrounded by them. I have a book Ma and Pa gave me when they discovered how much I enjoy books and how much I admire art work. It's called *Great Painters of the World*. It's a feast for the eyes."

"I'd like to see it." He sounded sincere, and she would gladly share her pleasure with him.

"Then you shall. Would you like to come back to the house and see it now?"

"I have to go to work. Mickey has plans this evening."

"Hmm. I wonder if his plans include Martha."

"I wouldn't be surprised if they do. I think he will be good to Jimmy."

"And to Martha, I'd hope."

He helped her to her feet, and they walked back as far as the manse. "I'll say goodbye here."

"Wait. Why don't you come by tomorrow and I'll show you the book?"

"I'd like that. After supper?"

"Perfect." She didn't realize until he walked away that it sounded like she wouldn't see him until then.

What did she expect? There was nothing more to do regarding the building project until the lumber and supplies came in. He had his work. She could use the time to prepare lessons. A kindly teacher back in Ohio had seen Victoria's interest in teaching and had encouraged it. Had even given her some useful books.

She had plenty to keep her busy until tomorrow evening.

The first thing she'd do was get *Great Painters of the World* from her trunk and try to guess what artists and paintings Reese would like best.

If the hours stretched before her like endless train tracks, it was only because she was anxious to see the school built.

Then what?

Reese would go to his ranch and she would start teaching. No doubt she'd see him on Sundays if he came to church.

It was for the best. He wanted something she couldn't give—the promise of forever.

She couldn't even promise it to herself.

Her lack of a past kept her from embracing the future. She could only take one day at a time, writing in her journals to make sure she didn't lose what she had. The chances of her recovering her memory grew less with each passing day, but she still wondered and feared if someone would recognize her. Surely not, after all this time. There had been a time she wished for it, searching every stranger's face for signs of recognition. Now she could think of nothing worse than having her life snatched from her.

A lump of unshed tears clogged her throat. She would not cry. Nor would she go running to Ma all fearful like she had when she was younger.

This was her life.

But one question blocked out all her firm admonitions.

How long was this her life? Would some stranger ride into town and know who she was? Would knowing her past turn her life upside down and sideways?

## CHAPTER 7

The next day, Mickey announced he had decided it was time to paint the barn. He handed Reese a bucket of red paint.

"I want the place to look nice."

"Any special reason?" Reese made sure to keep his voice casual. But he wondered if this decision to spruce things up had anything to do with Martha and perhaps a desire to impress the woman.

"Just figger it's time. There's a ladder in the back corner."

"I've seen it." He dragged it out and positioned it against a wall.

Mickey came out of his office. "Start on the side that faces the main street."

"Okay." Reese climbed down. "You wanting someone to notice what you're doing?"

Reese almost dropped the ladder on his foot at the way Mickey's face turned a dark red.

"Might as well make sure people can see it from the street," Mickey mumbled and went back inside.

Reese set the ladder, climbed up, and began to brush on paint. From his vantage point, he had a good view of much of the business section of town and many of the houses. If Sylvie discovered how well he could see, she'd spend all her free time up on a ladder. Good thing she was busy most of the day with her cooking.

Jimmy ran down the street with Spot at his side. He skidded to a halt and stared at a house.

Reese tried to see what had the boy's interest. He saw nothing and Jimmy raced away. Then a man Reese had seen at church and several times in town emerged, jamming his hat to his head with such fury that Reese gathered there had been a disagreement between the man and his wife. And Jimmy had overheard it.

The boy needed to allow people their privacy.

Reese painted as much as he could reach then climbed down to move the ladder. Again, he looked down on the town, though mostly he looked toward the church hoping to see some activity.

His wish was granted when Victoria and Eve appeared around the corner of the church and sat on the front steps. They carried on a lively conversation if the waving of arms meant anything. He couldn't hear them but saw they were laughing.

Jimmy trotted by and changed direction to join them. The three of them talked and laughed.

Reese sighed and turned his attention back to his job, slapping the paint on with more vigor than was called for.

Next time he looked toward the church, the three of them were gone.

No reason why it should make him feel lonely to see those empty steps, but it did.

What was he thinking? That Victoria could have a permanent place in his life? Besides her amnesia and his suspicion about her true identity, he could think of other reasons why it wasn't possible. Her heart was set on teaching. He would soon move out to the ranch he now owned. But most importantly, his heart was still locked tight. Betty had duped him. He didn't intend to open his heart to someone who could be snatched away.

What if Ma's letter informed him Miss Hayworth was safe at home? He'd asked after a letter yesterday but none had come in. He'd asked again this morning on his way back from breakfast at Sylvie's Diner. Still no letter.

He slapped on paint so hard it spattered on his face and he forced himself to calm down.

He painted all morning, relieved when he no longer had to climb the ladder but also disappointed because he couldn't watch people coming and going.

The sun was high overhead when Mickey took a horse from a rider and tended it for the bowlegged, white-haired man who said he had business in town. Reese watched the man walk away in a rolling gait common to older cowboys.

"You know that man?" Reese asked Mickey.

"Earl Douglas. He rides for the Bar K outfit. Comes to town from time to time. Why?"

"Just curious. Trying to get a handle on who lives around here." And because he was getting to be like

Victoria, and on her behalf, he was suspicious about every stranger.

"Fair enough. It's noon. Run along and eat and then take over here. I've got things to do."

"Let me clean up the paint things first." He had already returned the ladder to the barn. He put the lid on the paint, put the brush in a can of turpentine, and set it out of the way. He cleaned his hands and wiped them on a rag then trotted over to Sylvie's Diner.

Sylvie stood by the table of the same white-haired cowboy that had left his horse at the livery barn. She looked up at Reese's entrance and blushed.

Reese blinked. Another romance in town? It was enough to make him want to ride to his ranch before he fell into the same trap.

He sat at a table in the corner, smiling to himself. Betty had made him think romance was a trap. Victoria made him wish things were such he could freely court her, but how could he while he possibly had this huge secret about her? And him declaring he needed honesty.

Sylvie sat a cup of coffee and a plate of food before him. "I see you're painting the barn."

Reese guessed about everyone in town had seen the red paint by now. "Mickey says it's time to spruce things up."

Sylvie studied him. "He courting Martha?"

Reese sat back. "I can't say. Even if I knew it wouldn't be right for me to talk about my employer."

She huffed. "Just making conversation." She steamed away, but her bearing changed as she reached Earl Douglas's table.

Reese ducked his head to hide his grin. She would not

take kindly to him being amused at her interest in the old cowboy.

Reese's smile flattened. There was nothing amusing about the interest of a woman for a man, or a man for a woman. He'd learned that with Betty, who taught him it could be pretend and temporary. But sometimes it was real and lasted. He had only to look at the preacher and his wife to be certain of that.

But only if there was mutual trust.

He finished his meal and hurried back to the livery barn.

Mickey wore a new hat and departed as soon as Reese came into sight.

Reese checked on the horses in his care. He pumped more water into the trough and swept the floor of the office. He brought out a cart and fork and was about to start cleaning up the horse droppings in one of the stalls when Jimmy appeared with his dog at his side.

"Mickey said I could come help you."

"Grab a fork and start picking up the manure."

Jimmy hurried to do so and attacked the job with more enthusiasm than Reese could find. Which did not stop Jimmy from talking, Reese soon discovered.

"Mickey is building a new washstand for Ma. Says if he makes it the right height, her back won't hurt so bad." He shoveled a moment. "You think he's gonna ask her to marry him?"

Reese shouldn't have been surprised that Jimmy wondered about the man's intentions. "What would you think if he did?"

Jimmy leaned on the handle of the fork to consider

the question. Finally, he nodded. "I guess it would be okay. I'd be happy if Ma didn't have to work so hard."

It was a noble answer, but Reese wondered how Jimmy felt for himself. "You wouldn't mind having Mickey for a stepfather?"

"He's my friend, so I wouldn't mind."

"Good to hear."

They cleaned the entire stall.

"You want help painting?" Jimmy asked, his eager expression informing Reese the boy thought painting would be fun.

"Sure." He found a second brush and, side by side, they finished the one wall.

Jimmy went to the back of the barn. "I could paint from the ladder."

Reese shuddered to think of the boy up there. He shuddered again at the idea of Jimmy learning how much he could see from the vantage point. "It's getting on. I need to clean up." Mickey hadn't said when he'd return. Hopefully it would be soon so Reese could keep his appointment with Victoria. "You better get on home and see if your ma needs anything."

Jimmy raced away, Spot at his heels.

Reese cleaned up himself and the paint things. And then he waited. Unable to relax, he strode along the perimeter of the fence. Reached the street and turned back. He went to the side of the barn and studied the new paint. He went to the doorway and watched down the street.

His breath whooshed out when Mickey came into view, grinning widely.

## A LOVE TO CHERISH

He didn't wait for Mickey to reach the barn before he strode away.

Mickey called after him, "I see you're in a hurry to visit a certain young lady." The man's laugh held no malice.

Reese took a hard right. He'd almost forgotten to eat supper. He entered Sylvie's Diner, half expecting to see the old cowboy still there, seeing as he hadn't come back for his horse. But he wasn't. Reese took a seat. Sylvie hurried over with his meal.

"Thought Mr. Douglas might be here," he said, expressing only casual interest. But even so, Sylvie blushed furiously.

"Now why would you think a fool thing like that?"

"Only because his horse is still at the livery barn and this is the only place he'll find supper." He looked at his plate. "Supper looks good. Thanks."

She hovered at his side as if wanting to say something. Strange. He knew she wasn't a woman to mince words or consider them before she spoke.

Finally, she dropped her arms to her side. "Supper is always good." And she huffed away.

Reese ate his meal fast enough to make Sylvie raise her eyebrows.

"Eating like that could give a man indigestion, and then he'll blame my food when it's his own fool fault."

"I'd never complain about your food." He was about to push away from the table.

"I got some nice spice cake if you're so inclined."

Reese would have hurried away without the cake, but he had no desire to earn Sylvie's disfavor or any more speculation from her as to his intentions concerning Victoria. "I'd love a piece of cake."

She brought a slab as big as his fists, covered in a mound of whipped cream.

Seems he'd earned her favor.

Or maybe having Earl Douglas come by today had mellowed her.

He glanced at the clock and decided it was the right time to go to the manse—not too early so as to seem overly eager. Not too late so as to make Victoria think he didn't care one way or the other if he saw her.

He paid for his meal and strolled down the street. He went by way of River Street. The river was a hundred yards to his right bordered with trees in their fresh spring green. Businesses on his left gave way to homes. An older couple sat on the porch of one. Reese could feel them watching him until he was out of sight. Red and yellow tulips blossomed in another yard.

And then he reached the manse. Only a screen door shut the inhabitants inside. He heard Eve say something. Her ma replied. He strained to hear Victoria and then the girls began to sing. He paused on the step to enjoy their serenade.

"Company," Josie said, and the song ended.

Victoria swung the door open. "Coming in?"

He pulled off his hat and stepped inside. "I didn't want to put an end to the music."

Victoria quirked her eyebrows at the others, hummed a note, and they began singing again. She waved at him, inviting him to join in.

"Don't know the words," he mumbled, and sat at the table to listen and enjoy.

Little Blossom edged toward him until she leaned against his knees, facing him.

He smiled at her. She must have taken it for invitation, because she climbed to his knee. He adjusted her so she faced the trio, who continued to sing though they looked at each other as if seeing him hold the little girl meant something special. All he could say was it felt good to have Blossom lean against him.

The girls finished.

"Where's your brother?" he asked Blossom.

"Gone."

He wasn't sure what she meant, and the girls looked puzzled. "Where's your mama?"

"Sleeping."

Victoria bent to Blossom. "Did Donny go somewhere?"

"Out."

Mrs. Kinsley entered the kitchen in time to hear the child's reply. "I'll check with Stella." She returned in seconds. "She's asleep and there's no sign of Donny. Blossom, did he say where he was going?"

Her eyes wide, she nodded. "I not 'posed to tell."

"Was he going to the river?" It was the worst thing Reese could think of. He hoped to quickly eliminate that possibility.

Blossom nodded.

Mrs. Kinsley gasped. The three Kinsley girls looked shocked.

Reese set Blossom on a chair and planted his hat on his head. "I'll find him."

The water was high and fast from the spring runoff.

*Please, God, help him be safe.*

***

Victoria hurried after Reese. "I'm coming too."

They trotted across the yard, then the dusty street. They slowed as they reached the trees. He held back branches so they wouldn't slap her. She was breathless when they broke through the trees to the banks of the river. They looked right and left and didn't see Donny.

She looked at the river for any sign of the boy. "He's only five years old. If he fell in—" She couldn't finish. The child would be swept away in the icy waters.

"Donny," Reese called, making Victoria jump in surprise.

"Donny," she called.

They strained for any sound but heard only the water rushing by.

Reese jumped from the grass bank to the gravelly shoreline, held out his hand to assist Victoria.

"Where do we start?" she croaked.

"We'll head downstream. Maybe…"

He didn't need to say anything more. If Donny had fallen in, he would be carried in the current. Perhaps making it to shore at some point. She would not allow her thoughts to go any further.

The rocks beneath her feet made walking difficult and Reese reached out to take her hand. She clung to him, needing to feel his strength as much as she needed help to keep her footing.

They called Donny's name several times and paused to listen. They reached a place where the water churned over rocks.

Reese stopped. "If he was in the water, he would have

caught on these rocks. Let's search the trees. Though why wouldn't he answer us?"

"Because he's five. He might not have heard. He might be scared. He might be— I don't know. Any number of things." She tried her best to keep her voice steady but knew she failed miserably.

"We'll find him." Reese squeezed her hand, but he didn't smile.

She knew he was as worried as she, and for some strange reason that comforted her.

They climbed to the grass and called, slowly making their way back upstream.

Reese pulled her to a halt. "Listen. Do you hear that?"

She held her breath and strained to catch a sound. "Is it…? It sounds like someone crying."

Reese hurried into the thicket of trees. "He's here."

Victoria was on his heels and knelt before the little boy. "Donny, what's wrong? Are you hurt?" She felt his arms, his legs, and his head.

"I'm not hurt," he managed.

"Then what is it?"

"I'm sad. Pa is dead. Ma is sick. There's nothing to do, and I don't know where we live anymore."

She sat on one side of Donny, Reese sat on the other, and they put their arms around the boy. Reese's arm was warm and heavy on hers. A very comforting feeling. But she immediately dismissed the thought. This was about Donny.

"Your mama still has your farm, doesn't she?" Reese asked.

"I guess so. But she said we might not be able to keep it cause we aren't living there."

"It's a homestead," Victoria explained.

Reese nodded. "They were there until a month ago?"

She nodded.

"Then they're okay for now. Is someone putting in a crop for her?"

"Kade is taking care of the place."

"There you go, young Donny. You still have a home."

"But when are we going there?"

Victoria looked to Reese for the answer.

He was the sort of man who would comfort and support. Who would—

She forced herself to look away from his dark-eyed kindness. "It will be a little while before your mama is strong enough to live out there."

Donny hung his head. "I like the farm. I had a cat and a dog. Kade has my dog. Says he isn't a town dog. I used to chase gophers and grasshoppers and butterflies. Now mama says I must stay in the yard."

"Let's get you home before your ma starts to worry." Reese rose and pulled Donny up with one hand and Victoria up with the other.

They traipsed back to the house.

Donny's steps slowed as they reached the yard.

Reese turned the boy to face him. "If your mama agrees, I will take you out to see your farm. Me and Miss Victoria, if she is willing. How would you like that?"

Donny's eyes widened. "Really?"

"If your mama approves."

Donny flew toward the house. Almost went through the screen door without opening it.

"That is very kind," Victoria said, her throat threatening to close off at Reese's offer.

He grinned at her. "He's not a town kid, that's for certain. Will you come with us?"

"If my mama approves."

He chuckled at the way she imitated him. "We better go ask."

They laughed as they went into the house.

"I'm glad to see him safe and sound," Ma said. "But he raced into his mother's room before I could stop him. He's wakened her."

They could hear Donny talking excitedly and Stella's soft reply, then he dragged her down the hall and into the kitchen.

"Tell her, Reese," Donny said.

"Ma'am, I said I would take him out to your farm tomorrow if that's all right with you."

Stella looked relieved. "It's fine with me and thank you. The boy has been getting restless." She studied her son. "You're so excited, I don't suppose you'll be going to sleep any time soon."

"Eve and I will take him out," Josie said, holding her hand toward the boy.

He darted past them into the evening.

Ma laughed. "Now you and Blossom can rest. And I have some letters to write." Stella and Blossom went to the bedroom they shared. Ma went to the parlor to write her letters. That left Victoria and Reese alone in the kitchen.

She remembered why he had come. "I'll get my book. Wait here." She hurried up the stairs, grabbed her copy of *Great Painters of the World,* and returned to the kitchen to put the book on the table. He pulled a chair to her side so they could look at the pictures together. She suddenly felt self-conscious. Why did she think he would be interested in old art pictures? She'd once showed it to a young man back in Verdun who came often to the house and seemed to want to spend time with her. The young man —a boy, really—had laughed.

"What good are old pictures? Can't eat 'em. Can't sell 'em. Can't even hang 'em on the wall to decorate the place." He'd refused to look at more than the first page.

"Aren't you going to show me?" Reese asked as she hesitated.

"You might be as bored with them as Donny is with town life."

"Or I might be fascinated."

"Would you say if you were bored?"

"Do you want me to?"

She nodded. "Like you said, honesty is the best policy."

His eyes darkened. He opened his mouth as if he wanted to say something then seemed to think better of it.

She was about to ask him to speak his mind when he said, "I'll tell you either way."

"Okay." She opened the pages and told him about Leonardo da Vinci and Michelangelo. She paused, giving him time to say he was bored.

"Go on. It's fascinating."

She turned page after page. She knew the history of each painting and each painter. They came to the end and she closed the book. "What did you think?"

"I'm in awe."

"Is that good?"

"Yes. It's amazing to see how differently the artists see the world."

"What do you mean?"

"Take this, for instance." He turned the pages back. "The tree leaves have been replaced by angels. I will never look at trees the same again. And I will always feel there are angels keeping watch."

"What one was your favorite?"

He turned the pages. "This one. The lady with her arms full of fruit and sunflowers in her hair."

His choice surprised her. "Why?"

"Because of the bright colors and the bounty of produce. The whole picture is full of life and abundance. What's your favorite?"

"Two actually. Blue Boy and Pinkie."

"Why?"

She knew the answer, but it always left her feeling lost and afraid. "Because I remember them hanging on a wall when I was young."

"You mean before you lost your memory?"

She nodded, clinging to his gaze as if it would keep her from falling into the abyss of her unknown. "Why can I remember that? And the history of all this?" She tapped the book where it lay on the table before them. "I can remember how to play the piano and I have a vast store of knowledge that came with me." Shivers began in the depths of her being, but she had vowed she would stop letting fear of her past affect her so strongly and so negatively. She held her breath to still the tremors.

"Victoria, what if someone could tell you about your past? Would you like that?"

The abyss edged closer. "What if I remember my past

but forget now? Forget Ma and Pa and my sisters and even Josh?"

"What if you don't forget them?"

"Then I would be two people. I wouldn't know who I am." The shivers intensified.

"Isn't knowing better than wondering and being afraid?" He caught her hands. She hadn't even realized that they twisted round and round.

"I wish I could be certain of that, but I can't. No one can tell me what will happen if I learn my past."

He draped his arm around her shoulders. "It's all right. You're all right." He pressed his forehead to hers. "Things will work out when the time comes."

"When the time comes? What do you mean? Do you know something?" Her heart stalled partway through a beat.

"I mean that God is in control of your life, and you can rest in His love and care."

Her shoulders fell. The tension in her neck disappeared. She kept her forehead to his, absorbing his strength and comfort. "Ma taught me a verse that assures me of that. 'For I know the thoughts that I think toward you, saith the Lord, thoughts of peace, and not of evil.'" Her insides steadied.

He cupped his hand to the back of her neck. "That was one that Hoot taught me."

She chuckled softly. "Good old Hoot."

Laughing, he pulled her to her feet. "Let's go for a walk. There's nothing like a soft evening to calm a person."

She couldn't have agreed more and sorely needed to erase the strain of the last few minutes. She shivered.

Reese noticed and pulled her arm around his and pressed it close to his side.

What would she do if someone appeared who knew who she was? Would she have a choice in what happened, or would others decide her future?

Like she'd said to Reese, who would she be? Was it possible she might want to be the other Victoria?

## CHAPTER 8

*R*eese spent a restless night. He hadn't lied to Victoria but neither had he been completely honest, and it went against his own sense of right and wrong. But after hearing how upset she became at the idea of learning who she was, he was doubly convinced he must wait for the letter from his ma and speak to the preacher before he did anything.

Her father would be back Sunday. He'd talk to him then.

Reese did a few chores for Mickey then asked for the rest of the day off. "I'll be back to look after the place later in the day."

"Taking Miss Victoria out?"

"Sort of. Young Donny is homesick for their farm, so we're taking him there for a visit." He arranged for the use of a wagon then went to the store where he purchased some cheese, a loaf of bread, and got Norm to wrap up a handful of dill pickles.

"Planning a picnic?" Norm asked.

"If I'd been planning it, I would have asked Sylvie to put together something better than this." He explained that he was taking Donny to the farm. And Victoria was coming along.

Norm chortled. "Lisa is going to be pleased to hear this."

"Can't imagine why. Throw in a handful of peppermints too. And maybe some dried apples." They'd make a nice treat.

"Why? Because she'd been trying to get Victoria to move forward since the day they became friends."

"How's that?" He guessed he knew but he wanted to hear it in another man's words.

"The way Lisa explains it is Victoria seems stuck between a past she can't remember and a future she's afraid to count on. Glad to see you've convinced her to accept life as she knows it."

Norm lifted a hand as if an idea had surfaced. "There's a letter for you." He retrieved it from behind the wicket.

Reese looked at the return address though he had no need to. He'd be getting a letter from only one person. Ma. And the writing on the left-hand corner confirmed it. His heart thumped hard against his ribs.

"Ma has written," he said, keeping his voice steady. "Best see what she wants." He opened the letter and skimmed the newsy parts and reports about Ralph, his stepfather, until he saw the words he needed to see.

*Miss Hayworth is still missing. Ralph says Mr. Hayworth continually asks his employees if they know anything. But no one does. The young lady has vanished completely. I know her father had hired detectives to search for her. I can't understand why they can't find her.*

Reese's face was cold. Victoria had to be the missing woman. And he must carry the secret until he could speak to the preacher. This was not news he wanted to tell Victoria without having her surrounded by those who loved her.

Reese paid Norm and left the store, his conscience accusing him. Mr. Hayworth would have to be informed, and he would doubtlessly swoop in to claim his daughter. He would make accusations much like the ones he'd made at the foundry and generally turn Victoria's life upside down, but also the entire Kinsley family and likely, the whole town.

He wasn't offering Victoria the future so much as the past. Though she didn't know that. And he couldn't tell her just yet.

He pulled up to the manse and before he even set the brake, Donny ran toward the wagon. His mother stood in the doorway watching.

"You be a good boy, hear?"

"I will, Ma. I promise."

Victoria stepped from the house with a basket in her hands. Her hair was rolled softly about her head. She wore a pretty blue bonnet that matched her eyes. Eyes that smiled even when her mouth didn't. Her dress was a muted dark blue that on most women would look drab, but on her, it looked like a royal gown. Fit for a rich young woman.

Reese forced his thoughts into sensible trails. He got down and took the basket she carried. "What do you have here?"

"Lunch for us."

He chuckled and pointed to the paper-wrapped parcel on the wagon floor. "I put together a few things too."

"At least we won't starve."

He assisted her to the seat, resisting an urge to let his hand linger on her waist. Everything in him yearned to wrap this woman up and protect her, but he would be powerless once her father learned of her whereabouts. It still stung to remember the man's high-handed ways with his employees at the foundry after his daughter's disappearance. Reese knew he wasn't the only one who had felt accused and threatened by the man.

Did such a man deserve to know that his daughter had grown into this lovely young woman? Not that it mattered. He was Victoria's father, and *she* deserved to know.

They made their way south on River Street until they were out of town then followed the rutted trail further.

Donny sat between them, barely staying on the seat as he looked from side to side, pointing out familiar land marks.

"Pa showed me an owl nest over there. He lifted me up to look into the nest and laughed so hard he had to bend over 'cause I screamed when I saw the baby owls. They's all beaks and sharp claws." He held up his hands with curled fingers to illustrate. "Pa said the prettiest wild flowers were right over there."

Reese rumpled Donny's hair. "Why don't we stop there on the way home and pick a bouquet for your mama?"

"Oh yes. Mama would be so happy." He sat back,

sobered by something. "I think Ma misses Pa so much it makes her sick."

Reese glanced at Victoria over Donny's head. If he wasn't mistaken, her eyes glistened too brightly. It gave him a perfect excuse to reach over and rest his hand on her back.

She smiled at him as she spoke to Donny. "Your ma was real sick during the winter. It will take time for her to get better."

"I guess. Look. See that hill? Pa called it the Big Nose Hill. He said it looked like an old man's nose."

Reese and Victoria looked the direction Donny pointed. Reese laughed. "It does look like a nose. Your pa sounds like a very nice man."

"Yup. He sure was." Donny stood.

Reese caught him by the back of his trousers. "Hey, now. I don't want you falling out. Your ma would skin me alive if something happened to you."

Donny sat down. "Just trying to see the place. There it is." He pointed and bounced up and down.

Reese slowed as they approached the farm and let Donny jump down. The boy ran toward the barn yipping and yelling.

"You've made one little boy very happy." The approval in Victoria's voice felt like warm sunshine.

"It didn't take much."

"You're being modest. You had to give up your day to do this."

He hoped he managed to look sad. "Shucks. To think I could have been painting the barn. Have you noticed how red it is becoming?"

She chuckled. "It's pretty hard to miss."

They drew to a halt in front of the house, but he didn't make any move to get down. "Do you want to know what I learned while painting the barn?"

"Of course."

He leaned close and whispered. "From the ladder I can see most of the town and people coming and going."

"Why are you whispering?"

He looked to the right and left as if fearing someone would overhear him. "I don't want Sylvie or Jimmy to know it. They'd be up there all day long not missing a thing."

She laughed, the sound a breath of music. "I don't think they miss hardly anything as it is. We certainly don't want them seeing more."

"Can't hear too well up there though. I guess that's one disadvantage that might discourage them."

Her expression was sober, but her eyes sparkled. "I think we might have a little concern for Sylvie's safety. Would the ladder support her weight?"

"I don't think we want to find out." He jumped down and reached up to help her to the ground.

"Stella asked me to look around. I assured her Kade was taking good care of the place for her, but she said he's a man and might miss things a woman would see. She especially wanted to know that her house was all right."

They went inside.

"Wow," Reese said as he glanced around. "The place is as clean as Martha's laundry."

"I think Flora might have had a hand in this. I know most people look at her and shake their heads because she rides like a man, but she is a very caring person. Didn't take Kade long to realize that."

Victoria went to a bedroom, paused in the doorway, and then turned so suddenly he didn't have time to step aside. She bumped into him hard enough to make him grunt and treaded on his toes.

He caught her by the shoulders to steady them both.

"I'm sorry." She took half a step back. "Did I hurt you?'

He wasn't hurt, but he didn't intend to miss an opportunity to tease her. He moaned and grabbed at his foot. He hobbled to the kitchen and fell to a chair.

She leaned over him. "What can I do?"

Her face was so close to his he could see the way her eyelashes grew fair closer to her eyes, and dark at the outer edges. He could see a rim of darker blue around the iris of her eyes and the tempting softness of her lips.

Her eyes met his. The clock stopped ticking. Perhaps it never had ticked. But the silence of the clock was replaced by the steady beat of his heart against his ribs. Her gaze went to his mouth. His went to hers. He forgot his injured toe. Caught her shoulders and pulled her closer.

He wanted nothing so much as to kiss her, but he would not do so until he was able to be honest with her. He wanted nothing to do with a relationship that wasn't built on…what was the word he'd used? Authenticity.

He eased her back rather than forward.

"Is your foot okay?"

He reveled in the breathlessness of her question and got to his feet, testing his foot. "I don't think it was hurt too badly. Is there anything else you want to look at in here?"

She narrowed her eyes. "You let me believe I'd hurt you?"

He backed away as she stalked him. "I thought it might be fun. Maybe I was wrong."

She grabbed his shirt front. "You are certainly wrong about that, and many other things."

He caught her hands and held her at arm's length. Not because he feared her pretend anger but because he knew it would take only an inch closer and he would pull her into his arms.

He couldn't. Not when he held such a big secret. One that had such awful power to destroy her current life. And his too. He did not fit into a rich girl's way of life.

"What else am I wrong about? Do tell."

She pulled her hands free. "That will be my little secret." She dashed for the door, laughing merrily.

He chased her and skidded to a halt in the sunshine. He could not run after her, because if he caught her, he would surely forget all his good intentions. "Do you think we should check on young Donny?"

She was already on her way to the barn. He followed her into the dim interior.

* * *

VICTORIA BREATHED in the warm air, but it did nothing to still her racing heart. What had happened in the house? A momentary lapse of common sense. She'd barely stopped herself from kissing him and then from grabbing him and holding on.

She'd scared the poor man, and she couldn't blame him for his reaction.

Glad of a diversion, she stepped into the barn and called, "Donny?" They shouldn't have left the child unsupervised. Yes, he was used to this place and, from what he'd said, been allowed to run freely. But she couldn't help but think of the fright he'd given them yesterday.

"Shh." His voice came from a shadowed corner.

Reese at her side, they went to the boy where he sat cross-legged on the dusty floor. She knelt, saw what he held on his lap, and shuddered.

"What have you got?" Reese asked.

"Baby mice."

Four of them, squirming about.

"Aren't they sweet?"

Victoria pushed to her feet and again shuddered. Sweet was not the word she would use to describe the little creatures. There were only beginning to grow some fur and their eyes hadn't opened.

Reese chuckled. Saw the look on Victoria's face and came to her side. "They're harmless baby mice," he said.

"Mice are mice." She wouldn't say exactly what she thought of them with Donny obviously thinking they were nice.

"Can I take them home?" he asked.

Victoria gave Reese a pleading look. *Make him leave them here.*

He grinned.

"Now is not the time to tease me." Her voice croaked.

His grin widened. "Donny, they need their mama still. I'm afraid they'll have to stay here."

*Thank you,* she mouthed.

"I guess you're right." Donny set the little nest on the floor and ran from the barn.

Victoria's lungs released in a whoosh.

Reese, laughing, took her by the arm and led her into the sunshine.

She shuddered twice.

He draped an arm about her shoulders and tipped his head to hers. "They won't hurt you."

Her insides warmed at his comfort. "You can't be sure of that."

He grinned far too widely as they followed Donny.

The boy climbed over the fence and raced around the pen. He paused in front of Victoria and Reese. "Ma had to let the cow go but she said we'll get another one when the time comes." He circled the pen once more then left it to go toward the house where he kicked away some leaves. "It's here. My farm is still here. Come and see."

They joined him and saw that he had built a tiny farm with fences made of twigs. There was a small barn. "Pa made me this." He picked it up and carried it to the wagon then returned to dig some weathered carved animals from the covering of leaves. "I shouldn't have left them out. But I got sick and forgot them." He brushed them off and took them to the wagon.

Then when Victoria feared he might be overcome with sadness, he ran past the house toward the field. Kade had already put the seed in the ground, and Donny squatted to study the furrows.

"We might as well sit here where we can watch him." Reese pointed to the sunny spot next to the house and they sat down, side by side, elbows touching.

She knew she should put some distance between them, but the sunshine cocooned her in a state of inertia.

What would it hurt to let herself enjoy this moment of sweetness? She well knew it must be temporary.

Mustn't it?

Right now she couldn't answer her question.

They watched Donny go from place to place, exploring.

She was content to sit in the sunshine at Reese's side watching the boy and talking about ordinary things like the weather, the view of the mountains, and Donny's joy at being home.

Donny trotted up to them. "Are we gonna have a picnic?"

Victoria didn't realize how long they'd been there. "We brought food."

"I know the perfect place for a picnic. Mama and Papa used to take us there. You want me to show you?"

Reese got to his feet and pulled Victoria to hers. "Let's get the basket then you can show us."

Donny bounced impatiently as Reese trotted over to get the basket of food from the wagon.

Victoria chuckled when he picked up his package as well. "You're hungry?" she asked.

"I think young Donny is going to put away as much food as either of us. He hasn't slowed down since he got here."

"And he's not slowing down now." Donny had run to the top of a little hill and waved at them to hurry.

"Race ya," Reese said, laughing at her shock.

Victoria picked up her skirts and ran as fast as she could, but it was uphill and she wasn't a fast runner.

Reese waited at the top of the hill. "What took you so long?"

"I was being ladylike." She did her best to make it sound noble.

He laughed. "Let that be your excuse."

"I've never been a good runner. When the girls had any sort of race, I always came in last." She gave him a superior tilt of her nose. "I always said it's because I was raised to think running was not appropriate behavior. Of course, I don't know anything about my past so I can't say for sure, but I always thought it sounded reasonable. And convenient."

She'd expected him to laugh at her excuse, but any sign of amusement fled from his face as he turned away.

She caught his arm. "Why do you seem not to like my explanation?"

They followed Donny, who continued down the hill.

Reese shrugged. "It seems to me that your past has you trapped."

"Don't you mean my lack of a past?"

"Of course, I do."

"Funny, it didn't sound that way. Do you think I purposely avoid learning who I am?"

He stopped to face her. "No, but I do wonder how you'd deal with it if you were to find out who you were."

A slow burn began in the pit of her stomach and eased upward until she felt like her insides were on fire. The blaze raced to her brain. "I've told you why I don't want to find out my past after all these years. For one thing, why didn't someone try to find me? Someone besides my parents must have known of my existence." It was a pain that never healed, even though she thought it had been pushed into forgetfulness. Why couldn't she forget the things she wanted to and remember what she wished she could?

"Maybe they tried."

"Well, they obviously didn't try hard enough." She slipped past him to join Donny.

"It's right here," the boy said.

Victoria sucked in air to quench her anger and looked around. They stood on a slight slope that allowed them to see far to the west. "I can understand why your parents would come here. It's lovely."

"We sit there," Donny pointed toward some trees.

Victoria followed him and parked herself where he indicated.

Reese followed more slowly and lowered the basket and the parcel to the ground. "Victoria, I did not mean to upset you. I'm sorry."

She'd been trying hard to live fully the life she'd been given. To accept Reese's interest even though she felt like she walked into the dark by doing so. She'd let herself think it was safe because he made her feel safe, and now he'd made it seem like it was only her imagination.

"Well you did. I'm not stuck."

Except perhaps he was right. How could she not be? How could she have a future without a past? But discovering her past scared her so badly her mouth went dry. She would move on without a past. It was the only way. "I am Victoria Kinsley."

He studied her, his eyes dark with something deep that she couldn't understand.

"What else can I be?"

## CHAPTER 9

Reese settled on the grass beside Victoria. He could not keep his secret forever, and yet he feared to tell her. She got upset every time he came close to the subject. But he'd ruined enough of the day and meant to turn the mood back to cheerful, even tender, as it had been in the house. If he could only think of a way.

Victoria opened the basket. Both Donny and Victoria looked at him.

"I'll say grace." He snatched off his hat and tossed it to one side then said a few words of thanks.

Victoria pulled out thick sandwiches and handed one to Donny and then to Reese and took one herself. She kept her gaze on the distant mountains.

He thought of a verse she had quoted on that earlier walk. "'As the mountains are round about Jerusalem, so the Lord is round about his people from henceforth even for ever.' I remember you saying that verse to me." He waited, chewing slowly, hoping she would forgive him for upsetting her.

"'I will lift up mine eyes to the hills.'" Her voice was so low he leaned closer. She turned her face to him. She was mere inches away, close enough he could see a soft light in her eyes.

He knew before she smiled that she'd forgiven him. His heart threatened to burst from its moorings, and he ran a finger down her cheek. So soft. Like silk. "Thank you," he murmured.

Her gaze held his in a warm lock. "For what?"

"For forgiving me for being so insensitive." He drank in the sweetness of her eyes, the gentle curve of her mouth, and felt as if he had received a special blessing.

"Mama says I have to forgive." Donny's words ended the moment.

Reese looked to the child. "What do you have to forgive?"

"I have to forgive God for letting Papa die." The boy's voice quivered.

Victoria pulled him to sit between Reese and her. "Your mama is right. If we blame God for everything, we will end up a sorry mess."

"Kind of seems He could have stopped it."

"He could have, no doubt."

"Then why He don't?"

Reese waited for Victoria to answer the question.

"I don't have an answer for that. I only know if I don't believe in His love, that the world is a lonely, sad place." She caught Donny's chin and turned him to face her. "It's like those mountains. They are big and beautiful. They don't change. But there are days we can't see them. Days of snow or fog or rain. Does that change the mountains?"

Donny shook his head. "They're far away."

"God isn't though. He's as close as our breath and the air around us."

Donny considered it a moment. "Anyways, I forgive Him." He grabbed a handful of cookies and trotted down the slope to a gopher hill where he squatted down and whistled softly, no doubt hoping to entice a gopher to poke its head out.

Reese and Victoria looked at each other and laughed.

He grabbed a pickle, then lay on his back, a hand behind his head. "The sun feels good." He closed his eyes, the sun warm on his face, and turning the inside of his eyelids red.

An insect danced on his cheek and he swatted it away. It returned. He swatted again. And again. Only this time, Victoria's giggle gave her away. When the annoyance came again, he grabbed her arm, putting her off balance. She fell over him.

Her grin turned into surprise as she lay with her elbows jabbing into his chest. Her eyes darkened to midnight blue. She held his gaze, searching, until he felt as if she'd plumbed the very depths of his heart. Everything in him wanted to open himself wide, but he couldn't. He had a secret that lay between them as hard and unforgiving as a boulder.

A smile crept to her lips.

She tweaked his nose then pushed away, putting an arm's length between them. She broke off a piece of cheese and chewed it slowly.

He sat up. Took another pickle and bit into its crispy flesh. "The boy has more patience than I expected." Donny still sat by the gopher hole, waiting for a gopher to appear.

"Look," Victoria whispered, and jabbed her finger to the left.

Reese chuckled softly. Two gophers perched on their back legs a distance away, watching Donny.

Donny sighed and pushed to his feet. The two gophers scampered into their holes. The boy wandered along the foot of the hill, kicking at the grass.

"Is he looking for something?" Victoria asked.

"I don't know. Listen."

They both strained to hear the boy.

"He's singing." Victoria smiled at Reese. "I'd say that was a good thing."

Donny climbed the hill. "Can I have something more to eat?"

"Whatever you want." Victoria pointed toward the basket and the brown-paper wrapped package that lay open beside it.

Donny tore off some bread, took a piece of cheese and a pickle. "I'm gonna look for bird nests." He wandered into the trees along the side of the hill, looking upward for nests.

"Just a week until the school raising," Reese said. And then he'd have no more reason to hang about town. Did she realize that?

"I've been working on plans for lessons." She told him about a teacher she'd had back in Ohio who had encouraged her interest in teaching and taught her how to prepare to instruct a variety of grades. "I think I will have grades one to six if all the children are sent."

"You might have some big ones who can't read."

"I've thought of that and have been thinking of ways to interest them."

He listened as she talked about her plans. Her enthusiasm held his attention almost as much as the way her expression filled with anticipation.

Would all that be changed, perhaps her goals taken from her, when her parents learned where she was?

He wished there was some way he could keep her secret locked up inside him. But even if he did, how long would it be before someone else recognized her? How long before Smitty took matters into his own hands?

He'd sooner be the one to tell her who she was, with the support of her parents to keep her wrapped in their love. He'd let her be the one to decide if and when she wanted to meet her Chicago family.

He would have lingered all day, whiling away the hours in the sunshine, but Mickey was expecting him to take over the livery barn. "We should be getting back." He reached to gather up the picnic things at the same time she did. His hand covered hers on the handle of the basket.

They looked at each other. He knew from the shards of light in her eyes that she was as aware of the tension between them as he was.

He curled his hand around hers and drew her close. She lifted her gaze to his. If he wasn't mistaken, he saw there a world of invitation. Probably one she was unaware of and would deny.

Exerting every bit of self-control he could muster, he released her hand and finished gathering up the picnic things. He pushed to his feet, helped Victoria to hers, and smiled at her, not wanting her to think he didn't see her as the beautiful, alluring young woman she was.

They called Donny and returned to the wagon. Donny chose to sit in the back with his barn and animals.

Victoria sat beside Reese on the wagon seat. No one said anything for the first part of the return journey, which was odd for Donny, and Reese turned to check on him. The boy had curled up with his toys and fallen asleep.

Victoria had turned at the same time. Again, their gazes met. She smiled, and he felt a connection he could not deny. But neither could he act on it until he dealt with his knowledge of her past.

Sunday, he promised himself, he would find a time and place to talk to the preacher.

That left him three more days in which to keep his secret.

He thought Sunday would never come but now that it had, he wished he had a few more days before he had to deal with the information he carried like a lead weight. It was good that the past three days had been busy.

The school board members—minus the preacher—had met to discuss the school raising and how to proceed with the work. That took the most of one afternoon.

He spent two days painting the barn. The building looked good and from his vantage point on the ladder, Reese had enjoyed watching Victoria and her sisters work in their garden. He smiled to think of Donny's eagerness when they handed him a hoe and let him help.

Victoria had wandered by the livery one afternoon, supposedly on her way to visit Lisa. Mickey was away on business which happened to take him the direction of a certain widow by the name of Martha Anderson, so Victoria had kept Reese company for an hour before she continued on her way.

Saturday was busy with people coming and going. One notable visitor was Earl Douglas, who left his horse and said he hadn't had supper so went over to Sylvie's Diner. Reese might have found an excuse to call on the ladies at the manse. He could say he came to see if they needed wood chopped or water hauled. But Mickey asked him to stay and watch the barn.

But finally, Sunday arrived. He'd used the square washtub Mickey kept hanging on a wall and enjoyed a warm bath. He dried off, pulled on clean clothes, brushed his hair, and tucked in his new shirt—a handsome thing in light gray. Then he made his way to the church. Perhaps he could speak to the preacher before the service and arrange a time to talk.

He arrived at the church after the Kinsley ladies. They were already halfway down the aisle. He looked about for the preacher but didn't see him.

Victoria glanced back. She signaled him to join her.

He hurried forward to do so and slid into the pew beside her. "I don't see your pa."

"He's not here yet. Ma's getting a little worried. She keeps saying she doesn't know what to do if he doesn't show up." She slanted a teasing smile at him. "Maybe you could take his place."

He knew she was teasing and yet the idea drained the blood from his face.

She laughed softly. "Don't panic. I'm sure someone else will take his place. Someone who isn't going to pass out at the idea."

He forced himself to swallow past the constriction in his throat.

A gray-haired man dressed in dusty cowboy duds hurried up the aisle and paused near the front. He saw Victoria's ma. "Mrs. Kinsley?"

"Yes."

The cowboy sat in the pew in front of her and turned to speak softly. "Ma'am, I'm Jonathan Bates. Your husband has sent me with a message. He says Stewart isn't doing well and he can't leave him."

Mrs. Kinsley and her daughters gasped. "What are we to do?"

The old cowboy looked half fearful, half eager. "The preacher says one of the girls is to play the piano and the others stand by her and all of them sing. He says the congregation will enjoy singing with them."

"Does he expect them to sing for an hour?"

"He asked if I would tell what God has done for me, and I agreed."

Reese understood Mrs. Kinsley's consternation.

But for him, it meant he couldn't speak to the preacher about what he knew of Victoria.

How much longer must he wait?

\* \* \*

VICTORIA ACCOMPANIED her sisters to the piano and began to play. Flora had joined them. "Let's begin with number twenty-four," Flora said, and without paying any attention to the murmured surprise of those seated in the sanctuary, the girls sang one song after another. None of them had any idea how long they should sing, but after six songs, Eve whispered to them. "Let's make this the last one."

So, they sang the last song and returned to their seats.

There was a restless shuffling behind them then the old cowboy went to the pulpit. The place was immediately quiet.

"My name is Jonathan Bates. Most people know me as Bates. I have a ranch up near where Stewart Kennedy lives. That's where I met Preacher Kinsley and we got to talking. Well, Stewart Kennedy ain't doing so well. You could all remember to pray for him and the preacher. Anyways, when the preacher realized he couldn't make it this morning, he asked me to come here and tell you my story. So here I am." He cleared his throat and sucked in air.

"I was the worst man you could imagine. I done all sorts of things that would make you want to run me out of town, or worse, and I wouldn't blame you. Come a time I got sick of myself and the way my life was going. You might say I hit bottom and I hit it hard. Real hard. Weren't no place for me to go. Couldn't go up. Was as far down as I could go."

Victoria sat spellbound by the simple, heart-felt words of the old cowboy. She glanced around and thought from the way everyone stared forward that he had the same effect on the others.

Jonathan Bates continued. "While I was in the pit of despair, God reached down and plucked me up. I was lost but Jesus found me. Like the Good Book says, he found his poor lost sheep. He took me from the miry clay and put my feet on the solid rock. And there I will stay until He calls me home."

Victoria pressed her lips tight. *Lost but Jesus found me.* What beautiful words. Words she would carry in her heart every time she feared about her past.

"Now folks, you would think I would be happy as can be to have Jesus rescue me, and I was. But I clung to the old things. I hung on to the past. I was reluctant to let it all go. Lookin' back, I can't understand why I did. There was nothing back there for me. But it took a bit of struggle. Years, in fact, before I let it all go." As Bates talked Victoria felt as if the words were meant especially for her. She clung to the past and for what reason?

Bates wasn't through. "There was one more thing God had to do in my life. You see, folks, the thing that I blamed for setting me down that horrible path was the unfaithfulness of the woman I loved. The one I married and hoped to spend the rest of my life with. 'Stead she ran off with a carnival barker. I'm here to tell you, it hurt something awful. I let that bitterness grow into a festering sore. I let it drive me to do awful things. But here's the thing. She ain't now nor never was responsible for what I done. Those were my choices. So, when God said I had to forgive her, I knew I had to do it. Was it easy, do you think? You know what? Once I realized it was necessary, it weren't so hard. It was a relief, in fact. I'd been carrying around all that hateful stuff for so long and it was plumb tiresome. Folks, I'm here to say that when God sets a man free, he is free indeed. That's what happened to me and if it's helped you in any way to hear my story, I'm grateful to God. I guess I just want you all to know two important things. Jesus rescues the lost, and He forgives us of so much that any little bit of forgiveness He asks of us is nothing. God bless you all." He returned to his place in front of Ma.

No one moved. No one spoke. And then Ma stood and signaled the family to stand also. She turned to Mr. Bates. "Please join us for dinner." They left the church and, slowly, as if reluctant to end a meeting that had been unusual to say the least, the rest of the congregation followed.

\* \* \*

REESE STOOD outside in the sunshine. Bates's message had left him floundering. Was it as simple to forgive as the man said? Could he forgive Betty?

More importantly, would Victoria forgive him for the truth he would soon reveal?

Victoria misinterpreted his inaction. "You're invited to dinner as well."

"Thanks." He gladly fell in beside them. Told himself he regretted that he wouldn't be able to talk to the preacher about Constance Hayworth aka Victoria Kinsley. But in truth, he welcomed the reprieve.

A cowboy who had eaten with them on a previous occasion also joined them. Teller. Reese wondered if the man had his eye on one of the girls. So long as it wasn't Victoria.

It didn't take long for the family and their guests to sit around the table. Mrs. Kinsley asked Mr. Bates to ask the blessing.

The man's prayer was short, but Reese felt as if he'd been touched by angel wings. He wondered if any of the others felt the same. He hoped he would get a chance to ask Victoria and remind her of the picture of angels hovering above them.

Mrs. Kinsley asked for details about her husband and Stewart Kennedy.

"Stewart's wound has gotten infected. Your husband is applying compresses and doing everything he can, but he said he can't leave the man. Said Stewart needs his wound cared for but even more, he needs the preacher to pray over him."

"That was a lovely sermon," Mrs. Kinsley said. "I can understand why my husband asked you to speak."

"'T'weren't no sermon. Just telling what God's done for me."

Victoria leaned forward. "God has done much the same for me. I was lost after my accident. Didn't have a past or a memory. But God was with me. I've been found into this family where I know I am loved. I'm going to cling to that joy. This is the only family I have. I have to accept that any other family I ever had was killed in the accident."

Mrs. Kinsley dabbed at her eyes. "Victoria, you are as much my child as if I had given birth to you."

"I know." She squeezed her mother's fingers.

Under the table, Reese curled his hands into fists. Her family wasn't dead. He couldn't explain why they hadn't found her, but once they knew she was here, Victoria's world would be turned upside down.

He wished he could stop that.

Several of the others commented on Mr. Bates's talk.

Bates turned his gray eyes to Reese. "What do you have to say, young fella?"

"About what?"

"I don't know, but something has you squirming. Care to talk about it?"

Reese felt every eye turn to him. He widened his eyes, determined no one else would see how he struggled with his secret knowledge. "You make forgiveness sound easy." He hadn't meant to blurt out those words, but neither could he pull them back. He wasn't even sure he wanted to.

"I didn't mean to make it sound easy. It's not. But it's necessary."

"Why?"

Mr. Bates kept his gaze fixed on Reese. "Two reasons that I know of. God says if we can't forgive others, He can't forgive us. I expect you know the story of the unforgiving debtor. How his great debt was forgiven but then he demanded instant payment from someone who owed him a few pennies. God was not pleased with that man. But there's another reason. If we keep unforgiveness in our hearts it becomes a festering sore. For me, it made it so I couldn't love anyone else. Guess I didn't even much like myself." He smiled gently. "Forgiveness is a heart-cleansing for ourselves."

"I see." Reese's heart yearned for freedom from his anger toward Betty.

Donny edged forward. "Mama told me to forgive."

With a gentle smile, Bates asked the boy to explain.

As Donny repeated what he'd told Reese and Victoria a few days ago, Reese turned Bates's words over and over in his mind.

A little later, Victoria said, "I'd like to go look at the school site."

"I'll take you." He followed her from the table,

surprised none of the others joined them. But glad. "Did you feel the angels hovering nearby?"

She blinked. "Can't say as I did."

He told how Bates's prayer had reminded him of the picture in her art book.

"A comforting thought." They arrived at the school lot. She hugged her arms about her. "Just a two more days and a building will stand here. Norm tells me there are men building desks. Soon, very soon, I will have a classroom full of children." She faced Reese. "Mr. Bates made me realize I must let the past go, and I have."

"No more fears about someone knowing who you are?"

She shook her head. "I am Victoria Kinsley."

"And if someone does show up claiming to know who you were?" He had to do his best to warn her without alarming her.

She gave a dismissive wave of her hand. "I will still be Victoria Kinsley. Besides, I'm convinced I have no family. Otherwise, why haven't they come forward by now?" Her confident smile dipped into his heart. He could not say anything more until he'd spoken to her father.

"Reese, you need to forgive Betty, don't you?"

He wished he could deny it, but he couldn't. "I thought pushing it to the back of my mind was good enough."

"It's not, is it? I realized that today when Mr. Bates spoke of forgiveness." She looked to the treetops.

"Who do you have to forgive?"

"The man responsible for the train accident. Maybe even my first family, if I have one. Why didn't they look for me?"

"You don't know that they didn't."

"That no longer matters. I accept that I have no other family."

It was all Reese could do not to say she was wrong.

"What about you and Betty?"

He knew what she meant but wasn't sure it was as easy as she and Bates seemed to think. "Betty is history."

"I would argue otherwise if how she treated you is still affecting your decisions."

"She taught me to be cautious and that isn't a bad thing." His insides twisted as he thought of how Betty had made a fool of him. He thought of the key that locked his heart so solidly. Trust. He's always thought he needed to trust others. Now he saw it worked both ways. It pained him to know Victoria trusted him at the moment and yet he had such a huge secret.

"Is letting go so hard?" Victoria's words were gentle, drawing the poison from the wound Betty had left.

He sucked in air. "I forgive." The infection disappeared. He knew his face revealed his surprise. "Is it really that easy?"

She laughed and caught his arm to press her face to his shoulder. "I think we need to get to the place where we're ready."

He dipped his head to hers. "'If the Son shall make you free, you shall be free indeed.'" He would revel in the lightness of his heart except for the heavy rock of the secret he held.

Neither of them said anything more as they made their way toward the river and sat on the wooden bench overlooking the water.

Mickey and Martha walked toward them. Jimmy

trotted at their side, talking a mile a minute. From the other side, Flora and Kade, Eve and Josie, and even Teller came. Soon they gathered in a group and discussed everything from the weather to the upcoming school raising.

Reese would have liked to have Victoria to himself, but the burden of his secret weighed heavily, and he welcomed the presence of the others, making it impossible for him to spill what he knew.

He said goodbye shortly afterwards, leaving Mickey to enjoy the afternoon with Martha and Jimmy, and made his way to the livery barn.

The next day, the building material arrived. He and several other men trundled it over to the building site. Two of the board members stayed behind and they and Reese began to lay out the material, ready for the school to go up.

They worked until suppertime then returned to put in two more hours before dark.

Finished, they clapped each other on the back. "Tomorrow, we put up a school for Glory, Montana Territory. We're becoming a real town."

Reese made his way to the livery barn and retired to his room.

The school would soon be built. He'd have no more reason to stay in town. Except to talk to the preacher.

With every passing day, he wished he didn't have to tell Victoria what he knew.

Yet he couldn't wait to be shed of the burdensome secret.

CHAPTER 10

Telling Bates and then Reese about letting go of her past—the uncertainty and the worry, and yes, the wonder about why no family had found her—had left Victoria's heart soaring so high she couldn't stop smiling. Couldn't stop breaking out in song.

Josie sat on the edge of her bed. "Are you going to tell us why you're so happy? I can't remember the last time you were so joyful."

"What about Christmas? And when the folks told us we were moving?" It had been a relief to her to go further from where her accident occurred. There would be less chance of someone recognizing her and upsetting her life.

"Nope. Not half as cheerful as this." Josie leaned over to talk to Eve but made sure Victoria could hear. "Do you think Reese asked her to marry him?"

Victoria stared at her sisters. "Of course he didn't."

"Would you accept if he did?" Josie persisted.

"I don't...I can't." She sucked in air. She was Victoria

Kinsley. She would always be Victoria Kinsley. She wasn't going to let the past have any control over her. So she had decided. And yet the future frightened her.

Eve slipped to her side and hugged her. "I thought from what you said at dinner that you were free of your fears."

"I thought I was." She sniffed back tears. "It's easier to believe with my head than my heart." She tried to laugh. "But no, he didn't ask me to marry him. I expect he will go out to his ranch as soon as the school is up."

"It's not too far to ride into town." Josie said.

"Besides, you misinterpret my excitement. It's because tomorrow is the school raising. It's going to be a long day. We better get to sleep." She crawled into her bed, beside Josie, and forced herself to lie perfectly still though her insides tossed and turned.

Excitement about tomorrow. That's all it was.

THE GIRLS WERE UP before dawn to finish preparing food. They had fried chicken the day before and now baked biscuits. All the women would bring food for the men working hard at the building.

Ma glanced out the window several times. "I do wish your father would come, but I know he won't leave Stewart until he's sure the man is on the mend."

They ate a hurried breakfast, packed away the food to get later, then headed for the schoolyard. The streets were full of conveyances, horseback riders, and people on foot, all going the same direction. The schoolyard was crowded. Horses were tied nearby. Wagons lined the street.

Victoria, her sisters, and her mother joined the assembly, greeted by and greeting neighbors from far and wide.

Norm, as one of the board members, called for their attention. "Let us ask God's blessing and protection on our day." Men snatched off their hats. Women caught their children and hushed them, then Norm prayed. "Amen," he finished. "Now let's get to work."

The women sat on the ground in little circles so they could visit as they watched the work.

Victoria sat with her sisters, Lisa, and Lisa's sister, Annie, who was married to Norm.

Victoria observed how some of the men worked on the walls and another group constructed the rafters. Reese was in the latter group. Within minutes he had rolled up his sleeves. The morning was warm and the day promised to grow hot.

Jimmy carried a pail of water and a dipper to the groups of men.

Reese took the offered drink, lifted the dipper to his mouth, and glanced toward the women. His gaze skimmed the gathering until he saw Victoria. He smiled and touched the brim of his hat.

She gave a fleeting smile then shifted her gaze to the right lest anyone take undue notice.

A rider approached, one of the latecomers. She wouldn't even have noticed except she saw the way Reese scowled.

She turned to see who had earned such a dark look. It was Smitty. The man who had been at the manse for dinner a couple of Sundays ago. The man who asked her to accompany him alone. And then had stalked off as if offended by her hesitation.

Something about the man set her nerves into spasms.

The fact that Reese didn't seem to have a good opinion of him only intensified her aversion.

Just an ill-mannered cowboy, she told herself. She would be careful not to be alone with him. Having settled the matter to her satisfaction, she turned back to watching the construction. And if her attention centered mostly on Reese, no one need know.

He bent over to nail something. His arm swung the hammer, the muscles in his back cording. He swiped his arm across his brow to wipe away sweat then straightened to talk to one of the men.

She scanned the area to see where Smitty had gone. He stood with his arms crossed, observing those nailing together walls. Someone handed him a hammer and pointed him toward some work. She couldn't help but think he took his time about getting there. And even more time looking over the women.

His gaze stopped at Victoria. His expression gave no clue as to his thoughts and yet she shivered.

She turned away so she wasn't looking directly at him but didn't let him out of her sight.

Smitty sauntered over to talk to Reese.

Reese shook his head and continued to work, ignoring the other man.

Did Reese know Smitty? Under what circumstances?

Smitty wandered away, swinging the hammer but doing nothing useful with it.

Then Reese called for attention. "The walls are ready. Let's get them up."

The men lifted walls, fixed them in place, and braced them. Then one by one the joists went up. By the time the sun was directly overhead, the building had shape and form.

Victoria watched the progress with great interest.

"They'll soon be taking a break," Ma said. Long trestle tables had been set up to the side.

"I'll go get the food," Victoria said. She hurried down the street toward the manse.

She heard footsteps behind her. They seemed too heavy to belong to one of her sisters, and she turned to see who it was.

That man. Smitty. Why was he following her? She should have made certain someone accompanied her. It was too late now. She hurried onward, determined to reach the house and safety before he caught up to her.

Behind her, the footsteps increased in pace as well.

*Help.* She should not have left without one of her sisters, but Glory had always been so safe they never feared stepping out alone.

She passed the church. A few more steps and she would reach the safety of the house.

"What's your hurry, Miss Kinsley?" He was so close she could have reached back and caught a handful of the air around him.

She continued onward, determined not to show any fear. "I have to get the food and take it over."

"Maybe you'd like some help?"

Innocent words, but somehow making her feel threatened. "No, that's fine. My sisters will be here in a minute. And Ma."

"Ya don't say."

She reached the door, flung it open, and stepped inside. But when she tried to slam it shut, a booted foot stopped her.

"You ain't bein' very friendly. That's not nice. I'm just wanting to get to know you better."

"Fine. I'll be back at the grounds with the food." She did not mean the words as an invitation and kept her shoulder to the door so he couldn't push it open any further.

Josie and Eve came into sight behind the man.

"Here are my sisters now."

He shrugged. "I'll see you later." He withdrew his foot and strode the opposite direction of the girls.

They rushed to Victoria. "Who was that? Seems he was being rude and bold." Josie sounded ready to hunt the man down.

"You remember Smitty? The cowboy that was here a couple of weeks ago."

Eve shuddered. "I didn't care for him then and I care for him even less now."

"Me too." Victoria shuddered. "He scared me."

"What did he want?" Eve asked.

"To be friendly."

"A little too friendly, I'd say." Josie handed Victoria the platter of fried chicken. They each took something and headed back to the schoolyard. "Stick close to us," she said. "We'll protect you."

Eve chuckled. "I'll let Flora know. She'll scare some sense into the man."

Victoria laughed. "Maybe I was overreacting." But she didn't think so, and the way Josie and Eve looked at her, she knew they didn't either.

The tables were laden with food. The women and children gathered to one side. Ma spoke to Norm and he called for the men to halt work. He said grace and then the men helped themselves to food first so they could get back to work as soon as possible. The women would eat afterwards and take their time, glad of the chance to catch up on news from their neighbors.

Another late arrival rode toward them.

Victoria was glad to see it was Mr. Bates though she would have sooner seen her pa.

Mr. Bates went to Ma. "Your husband sends his regrets that he doesn't feel he could come but says to inform you that Stewart is on the mend."

"Praise God," Ma said. "Please help yourself to some food."

"Don't mind if I do."

Victoria's tension disappeared. Something about that man filled her with peace.

The men filed by as they filled their plates. Smitty looked at her and grinned.

She shuddered.

Reese watched, his expression tight.

She hoped he didn't think she encouraged the man. She stepped back, hoping to disappear into the midst of the women.

Donny caught her arm. "Where's Mama?"

"She's sitting over by the trees." Ma had brought a chair out so the woman could rest and yet be part of the activities.

"But I can't see her."

"Come on. I'll take you to her." She took Donny's

hand and they skirted around the crowd toward the spot where Stella sat.

Donny saw her and ran to join her. Stella kissed the boy on the top of his head and smiled at Victoria. Someone had taken food to Stella and Blossom. A third plate waited nearby for Donny.

Satisfied they were taken care of, Victoria turned, intending to return to the others.

She drew up short at Smitty directly in front of her.

"I only want to be friends," he said, but his voice slithered through her.

"I want to rejoin my ma," she said.

"Your ma won't go anywhere without you. Now why don't you come for a walk with me and tell me all about yourself?"

She fled, right back to Josie and Eve.

Eve grabbed her arm. "You look like you've seen a wild bear." She looked the direction Victoria had come. "Him again." She grabbed Flora and they bore down on the man.

Victoria almost laughed when he scurried away to join the men who had returned to the work.

\* \* \*

REESE WATCHED Smitty follow Victoria when she went to Stella. He clenched his fists. He did not want to be associated with the man, but he would not stand by and let Smitty make her life miserable. He took two steps toward them when someone called for him to hold the end of a board. He couldn't walk away. When he was free, he saw Flora and Eve headed toward Smitty.

A LOVE TO CHERISH

He chuckled as Smitty hurried to join the men.

The work demanded many hands, but he would gladly manage without Smitty's help. He went around to the far side of the building where Smitty stood watching.

The outer walls were being put up.

Reese grabbed a hammer and went to Smitty. "What are you doing here?"

"Helping with building the school. Just like everyone else."

"Except everyone else is actually doing something." He handed Smitty the hammer. "And they aren't bothering the Kinsley girls."

Smitty snorted. "Only, one of 'em ain't a Kinsley."

"You can't be sure and until you are, best you keep your suspicions to yourself."

"Ya think I'm going to stand by and let you claim that reward all to yerself?" He snorted again and walked away to pound in a few nails. Then he dropped the hammer, returned to his horse and rode away.

Reese ground his teeth. He should have been relieved, but he wasn't. How long did he have before Smitty took action toward gaining the reward? Reese didn't want it. But more importantly, he didn't want Mr. Hayworth riding into Victoria's life and upsetting it. But he couldn't be part of dishonesty and knew the truth must be revealed.

He returned to his position at the wall, driving home nails with three hard blows, sending shock waves to his shoulder.

The walls grew higher. A ladder was placed at one end.

Someone went to fetch another ladder to place at the

other end. As soon as they were ready, two men would stay up there and nail the boards in place.

"Jimmy!" A woman's sharp call caught everyone's attention.

Reese jerked around and saw Jimmy at the top of one of the ladders, hands pressed to the wall to balance himself. How had he climbed that high and why? He wobbled. The ladder shifted.

It was going to tip over and bring the boy crashing to the ground.

Reese leaped forward as the ladder tipped his way. He estimated he was about where the boy would come down and reached up to grab him. Jimmy landed in his arms, knocking Reese off his feet. He fell to his bottom. Jimmy rolled off.

"Heads up," someone called.

Reese looked upward. The ladder came straight for him. He scrunched his eyes and tipped his head. The ladder hit him hard. He saw stars. And then everything went black.

Someone placed a wet cloth on his head. Icy as if dipped in the river. He opened his eyes.

Mrs. Kinsley knelt over him. "Good to see you're conscious. But you had quite a blow to your head."

"I'm all right." He sat up but had to close his eyes and bite back a groan. He felt his head. "Ouch. How's Jimmy?"

"He's fine."

"Good." His head protested the sound of his own voice.

Victoria knelt before him, holding out a cup of water. "A drink might help."

He took the cup and drained it. Tried to focus on her

face, but he could only do so by closing one eye. "You look worried."

"You might say so. You could have been seriously injured. Maybe you are."

"Just a knock on the noggin. Good thing I got a hard one."

"I'm here to inform you that a knock on the noggin as you call it can radically change your life."

He wanted to reassure her and smiled. Ohh. That made his head hurt. "I'm fine. Time to get back to work." He pushed to his feet and wavered like a tree with its roots cut off.

"I think you should sit for a bit." Victoria took his arm on one side, Norm on the other, and they guided him away from the building. It took little urging to persuade him to sit down. He pulled his knees up and rested his chin on them.

Norm studied him a moment, shook his head, then turned back to the men who stood around watching to see that Reese was okay. "Let's get back to work."

Victoria sat on one side of Reese, Mrs. Kinsley on the other. His personal bodyguards, he thought with a mix of amusement and gratitude.

Martha Anderson and Jimmy stood in front of him.

"Jimmy, do you have something you want to say to Mr. Cartwright?" Martha asked.

"Yes, Ma. Reese, I'm sorry I climbed the ladder and was the cause of you getting hurt. Thank you for catching me."

"Glad I was there," Reese said.

"Thank you for saving my boy." Martha's voice carried a hefty dose of tears.

"Glad I was there," Reese repeated.

A few minutes later, Mickey came to Reese. "You saved the boy. Thank you."

"Glad I was there." He couldn't think of anything other than those words.

Sylvie came by. "There'll be an extra big piece of pie for you next time you stop in."

"Thanks." At the moment he wasn't a bit interested in pie.

Several others came by to offer gratitude.

Victoria leaned around him to speak to her ma. "Ma, make them leave him alone until his head stops swimming."

"I can try." Ma waved away the next person to approach. "Later, when he's feeling better," she said, so as not to offend the person.

"How did you know my head is swimming," he murmured to Victoria.

"Because of the way you keep one eye closed when you look around."

"Huh." He tried opening both eyes and thought better of it. "I should be helping."

"Seems to me you did more than your share by saving Jimmy."

"Huh."

After a bit, the dizziness disappeared. He could keep both eyes open and sat up to look around. The walls were almost up. Windows were being placed in one wall. The roof was done, and men laid the shingles on. "It's almost done. How long have I sat here?"

"Oh hours and hours and hours." Victoria spoke so

airily he turned too quickly to look at her and his head reminded him to slow down.

"I'll see if there is enough food left for supper," Mrs. Kinsley said, and joined several other women around the long trestle table.

"Are they going to finish today?"

"I believe they are."

"You'll be glad."

"Glad about the school and equally glad Jimmy and you are both alive."

He mused over those words. Wasn't sure he liked being on the same level as a building, even if it was new. "How glad?" He shifted so he could look at her without turning his head.

"What do you mean?"

"Do you think maybe I deserve some sort of thank-you gesture for all my hard work?" Then, lest that wasn't enough to make her agree, he added, "And for saving Jimmy."

"I'd say you do, but what do you have in mind?"

He chuckled but stopped immediately when his head protested. "Don't look so worried." He knew exactly what he wanted her to do. "I promised Donny to take him to the ranch. Come with us." He'd like one more outing before he had to tell her the truth about who she was.

"I'd like that. When?"

"Tomorrow?"

"What about your head? Don't you think you should wait a day or two?"

"My head is fine." He bounced to his feet to prove it

and forced himself to hold steady as the world turned around him. "Tomorrow then?"

"Only if you're up to it."

"I'll be up to it." He trotted over to grab a hammer and help with the school. And if he had to squint to see the nails he pounded in, no one seemed to notice.

Tomorrow he'd be well enough to go if he had to drive with one eye closed.

## CHAPTER 11

Victoria was more anxious to see Reese's ranch than she cared to admit. She even allowed herself to think he had invited her to see it because he wanted her opinion. Perhaps he wondered if she could see it as a future home for herself.

She shivered as much from anticipation as fear. She had determined that her non-existent past would no longer have a hold on her. It would no longer be allowed to dictate how she lived her future. So long as Reese could accept the chance that someone from her former life could show up and reveal it to her….she shuddered. So many scenarios had played through her mind as to what that life had looked like.

She was ready to go right after breakfast. "He might not take us," she told Donny who waited at her side. "His head might be too sore."

"A wagon's coming," Eve said from her station by the window. "He doesn't look any worse for his accident."

Victoria remained at the cupboard by the picnic

lunch she'd made. She didn't know if he would expect or even want one, but they would likely be gone past noon.

"He's getting down. Moves all right. Guess he's fine." Eve kept up her commentary until Reese reached the door, and then flung it open before he could knock.

"Howdy," he said. "How is everyone this morning?"

"We're fine," the three girls chorused.

Ma gave Reese close study. "Are you sure you're up to this trip? I wouldn't want to think of you collapsing out at the ranch and my daughter having to deal with that."

"Ma," Victoria scolded.

"I've got a lump on my head but nothing I can't deal with. No pain. No dizziness. Both my eyes are working." He widened them and leaned toward Ma to prove his point. "See anything wrong with them?"

"Oh you." She laughed and pushed him away. "Just take care of yourself and these two."

"Ma'am, you can count on it." He turned to Victoria. "Shall we?"

Stella hugged Donny goodbye, warned him to be good, and thanked Reese for entertaining her boy.

Victoria grabbed the picnic basket.

Reese took it from her and set it in the wagon. Donny sat in the back with a few of his farm animals to amuse him.

They rode out of town. Several people waved as they passed.

"The whole town will know where we're going before we get two miles down the road," Reese said.

Victoria laughed. "They're just concerned that you might be overdoing it."

"Well, I don't mind their interest and concern. It's

kind of nice." He leaned back.

She studied him. By all appearances he seemed relaxed, but she detected a tightness at the corner of his mouth.

He turned to her. "What?"

"You're worrying about something."

He blinked. "Why would you say that? Do I have a sign on my forehead?" He scrubbed at the skin there.

"No, silly. It's written right here." She touched the corner of his mouth. At the jolt that ran up her arm, she knew she shouldn't have done it.

He caught her hand and held it near his chest. "I think you're making that up." He slowly released her, and she sat up prim and proper as her ma would expect.

"We are now on my land," he said after a bit.

She looked about. "How can you tell?" Far as she could see, there was only more grass, more rolling hills.

"I have a special sense about it." He grinned, and she knew he was teasing.

"Like the lines that inform me you're worried. Care to tell me what's on your mind?"

"Umm. Well, there are a lot of things. Like how long will your pa be gone?"

That seemed a strange thing to concern him.

"Or whether or not Mickey and Martha will tie the knot. And then there's Sylvie and Earl. By the way, what do you think of that pair?"

"I know you're avoiding giving me an honest answer, but I have no desire to ruin a perfectly good day, so fine. Sylvie and Earl seem like a fine match. Only one problem."

"What's that?"

"Will she give up her diner or will he give up his job on the ranch?"

"That is a fine dilemma."

The lines at the sides of his mouth deepened. What was there about Sylvie and Earl that bothered him? "If she gives up the diner, I suppose cowboys like you might not have a place to eat when you're in town."

"That's sad to think of." He brightened. "But likely someone else will run her business. Maybe one of the Kinsley girls."

"Not me. I'll be teaching school."

Again, those lines deepened.

* * *

Reese pulled in his bottom lip, hoping it would make those lines Victoria referred to disappear. How ironic that she asked the question that he wondered about. Even if Mr. Hayworth didn't whisk Victoria back to Chicago, would she leave teaching to become a rancher's wife?

Not that he needed the answer, because he knew what Mr. Hayworth would do.

But he had until Mr. Kinsley returned, and he meant to make the most of every day.

He pointed out the hollows with lush grass, the trees that would provide shelter, and the rolling hills that allowed for good grazing. He pulled to a stop. "There it is." His throat tightened at the overwhelming sense of pride and ownership.

She studied it a moment then nodded. "Let's see it closer up."

Donny leaned forward. "This your place?"

"It is."

"Almost as nice as ours."

Reese glanced at Victoria and they shared a little smile.

He drove toward the house. Abe stepped out. "Good timing. I'm ready to leave. Could get on the trail this morning."

Reese helped Victoria down while Donny jumped out on his own.

Victoria stepped forward. "I don't know if you remember, but we've met. I'm sorry about your loss."

Abe nodded. "Thanks. How's your parents and sisters?"

"We are all fine."

Abe led them to the house. "Reese, I got things all sorted out." They stepped inside. "I'm leaving all this for you."

The house was fully furnished.

"Did you take anything?"

"Just personal things and my wife's rocking chair. They're all stored in the barn loft out of your way."

"I'll take care of them until you get back."

"Just happy to have things sorted out. My bags are packed. I would have left already but there's something been bothering the cows. Can't say if it's a bear or a cougar but I've been spending the nights out there, building a fire in the hopes of scaring off whatever it is. Been keeping the herd together. But now you're here, I'll be on my way." He trotted to the barn and emerged a few minutes later riding one horse and leading another carrying packs.

Reese was glad to see the man eager to move on but had hoped he'd stay a bit longer... at least until Reese had dealt with the truth he must reveal. But today would be his last day. He wouldn't be able to stay in town with his cows needing his care.

They watched Abe ride down the road. Then Reese turned to Victoria. "Would you like to see around the place?"

"I would."

He gave her a tour of the house. The roomy kitchen, the cozy sitting room where a family would spend long winter days, three bedrooms, two with beds and the third with a crib bare of bedding. Seeing that little cot tugged the cords holding Reese's heart. Abe had built this home with so many hopes and dreams.

They returned to the kitchen.

"It's a lovely home," Victoria said. "I can see his wife's touch in so many places." She ran her finger along the smooth table top. She glanced out the window, her blue eyes reflecting the cloudless sky. The skirt of her dark blue dress fluttered from the breeze through the open door. She'd removed her bonnet, leaving her head uncovered. Her blonde hair glistened as if touched by sunlight.

Reese knew that picture would stick in his mind forever.

"Can we look outside now?" Donny asked.

"Yup. Let's go." The three of them trooped outdoors. They wandered through the barn, now empty. They opened the doors of the outbuildings. Victoria exclaimed over the smokehouse and empty chicken house.

"This was her garden," Victoria said. "Look, there's even a few volunteer plants coming up."

"And a good crop of weeds."

Donny found a bent spoon and began digging in the soil.

They left him there and continued to wander around the place.

The sun was high overhead when Reese looked for a place to have their picnic. They could have eaten inside the house, but he wanted to find a special spot like Donny had at their farm. A place where he would go and remember this occasion.

Donny ran up to them. "I'm hungry."

Reese laughed. "Me too. Let's have a picnic." The three of them returned to the wagon and got the basket. "Wait while I get a blanket from the house." He dashed inside and grabbed one off the nearest bed. As he went through the kitchen to return outside, he glanced out the window by the table. The grassy ground dipped toward a little grove of trees. The perfect place for them to enjoy their food. A place he could see from the table.

He led the way to that spot and spread the blanket. He waited until Victoria chose where to sit and then he sat beside her, breathing in the scent of wild flowers and green grass.

"You gonna pray?" Donny asked.

Reese tossed his hat to the side and closed his eyes. His thoughts crowded with so many things. The desire to make this moment last forever was uppermost, warring with the way his conscience accused him of being like Betty.

The difference was his feelings were sincere. Only the circumstances of the situation were wrong. He said a quick grace then took a sandwich Victoria offered him.

He lingered on the taste of the fresh bread and how her eyes flashed with sunlight. He grabbed every moment of the day. The way she brushed her finger across Donny's nose to wipe away a bit of dirt. The way she laughed at Reese's teasing. The way she closed her eyes and lifted her face to the sun.

He could ask her to marry him. If she agreed, it would stop Mr. Hayworth from taking her back to Chicago. Only he couldn't be sure it would. Mr. Hayworth expected people to do as he ordered.

But the biggest reason he couldn't ask her was she needed to be free to discover who she was and how she wished to deal with that.

He wanted the day to last forever. Wanted to fill it with memories to last a lifetime. It made him think of something he had not thought of since it happened.

Leaning back, he said, "Once upon a time I remember being happy and sure the world would never change. I thought life was roaming the hills, exploring the beach, running across the yard to see my grandparents. It was idyllic. Then it ended. Abruptly. I was five years old." Donny had wandered away, so he felt he could tell Victoria the painful memories. "Everyone was very sad. I didn't know why, and then they took me to see my grandparents. Only they weren't smiling and hugging me. They were laid out in black clothes, stiff and waxy looking. I wanted to know why they looked that way and Mama said they were gone.

"That didn't make any sense. I could see them. Mama said they were in heaven and before I could ask how that could be Pa told me to hush. People came. Some patted my head. Everyone whispered. And then everyone was gone. Even Gramma and Grampa. And then Pa said we had to leave too. I didn't understand. Mama and Pa talked behind their bedroom door but I heard them.

"My pa sounded very angry. He said Grandpa had promised him the place but now he'd given it to the church. His voice grew louder as he asked what we were supposed to do?

"I couldn't hear what Mama said, only her pleading tone. Then Pa spoke again. I'll never forget his words.

"'I trusted them. If you can't trust your own parents, who can you trust? Aren't they supposed to love you and honor their word?'

"I was so frightened. Remember, I was only five. But if Pa was right and a person couldn't trust their parents, then what would become of us? Well, we moved to the city. Pa worked at the foundry and drank too much. He died. And Ma remarried." He stopped, shocked that he had said so much. He didn't even know he remembered it.

"Reese, that's a sad story. No wonder you expect honesty and trust between people."

"It wasn't all bad. I saw the mighty hand of God in my travels. In the land, in the storms, in the newborn calves, and in good people. I decided I would choose to trust Him. And not rely on others for my happiness."

She twisted a blade of grass. "Doesn't seem to leave much room for a wife and family. Don't you want that?"

He'd like home and family such as he'd known when his grandparents were alive. Full of welcome, warmth, and love. But all that required honesty, and he couldn't give her that at the moment.

\*\*\*

VICTORIA GATHERED up the picnic things. Reese had been distracted since they'd reached his ranch, and she understood. "I know you're anxious to be able to check on your cows. It's been a very pleasant outing and I shall cherish the day, but you need to take us home now so you can be a rancher." Meaning to tease him, she laughed, hoping he didn't hear the reluctant note amidst the merriment.

Reese took the picnic basket. "I hate to eat and run, but you're right. I have to take care of my cows."

They were soon on their way back to town and passed the time talking about things that didn't matter. The trees, the mountains, the sunshine...

Victoria ached inside, wishing for a reason to make the afternoon last even while knowing she couldn't. Reese must get back to his cows. He likely wouldn't be coming to town any time soon if his herd needed close watching. Even now, she felt his restlessness and knew he was anxious to get back to the ranch. She understood. She truly did. But she didn't want to say goodbye.

They drove down the street past White's Store. A stranger stood on the step momentarily then ducked inside. Not the usual kind of stranger. This was a city man, his suit and bowler hat giving it away. Victoria paid him scant attention as her mind raced with all the things she ached to say to Reese. But he'd given her no indication that he shared her growing affection.

They arrived at the manse and Donny jumped down, racing to the house.

Reese helped Victoria to the ground.

They stood facing each other.

"I don't know when I'll be back." He sounded regretful that he couldn't promise a date for returning.

"I understand." She pressed her hand to his forearm. "Be careful around whatever wild animal is out there. I wouldn't want to see you hurt."

He touched her hand and smiled.

Dare she think his eyes contained a thousand promises?

"I'll be careful. I will be back." He climbed to the wagon seat and flicked the reins.

She waited, watching as he drove away.

Just before he went out of sight, he turned, smiled, and waved.

Cherishing the thought that she would see him again, she went inside.

Ma rushed to her. "I'm so glad you're back."

Something in Ma's voice sent alarm bells ringing in Victoria's head. "What's wrong?"

Eve and Josie hovered close. And Lisa was there.

"What's going on?"

Everyone talked at once. "Someone has been asking some very strange questions about the family." "He asked everyone, even Jimmy."

Victoria sank to a chair, her heart thumping madly. "A city man?"

Lisa nodded.

"I think I saw him." She shivered and wished she'd paid more attention to the man. "Did he say what he wanted?"

Again, it was Lisa who answered. "Norm asked him, but he wouldn't say. His questions were unusual for a stranger. I heard him ask where the Kinsleys came from.

Were all the girls adopted?" She leaned closer and lowered her voice. "He showed Norm a picture and asked if any of the girls looked like that."

Victoria's heart slammed her ribs. "Was it one of us?"

"I didn't see it and Norm wouldn't say. He told the man it could be anyone."

"I don't like it," Josie said. "Come on, Lisa. Let's find this man and ask what his business is."

The two girls headed for the door.

"You be careful," Ma said, but she didn't ask them not to go. Which convinced Victoria her mother was as worried as she was.

"Ma, it must be someone from my past." She couldn't keep the tremors that filled her from shaking her voice.

"Let's wait until the girls get back."

Eve drew her mother to a chair. "I'll make some tea. You both look like you need something to calm you."

"Thank you, dear," Ma said, but Victoria knew tea would not still her fears.

Eve filled the kettle and waited for it to boil. She was pouring water over the tea leaves in the brown teapot when Josie and Lisa rushed in.

"He's gone," they announced.

The air whooshed from Victoria's lungs so fast that she felt weak. "Thank goodness." Eve served the tea. A warm, soothing drink to calm Victoria's nerves.

Who was the man and why was he interested in her? Was it as she had always feared…her past coming back to destroy her present and rob her of a future just when she'd begun to allow herself to dream of one?

## CHAPTER 12

Sunday morning dawned and Victoria was finally able to breathe a little easier. There had been no further sign of the man asking after her, and she allowed herself to think whatever he sought, it wasn't her.

Pa rode in after breakfast and Ma rushed out to hug him. He swept her off her feet and kissed her soundly despite Ma's protests that the girls were watching.

"I missed you," Pa said. He smiled lovingly at Ma for a minute then looked at the girls. "All of you."

As Ma fixed him breakfast, Pa told that them that Stewart was over his infection. "He's getting around a bit. I don't have to be there all the time though I promised I'd be back every few days to check on him. Now, what's new around here?"

Ma put a plate of food before him. "A man was in town asking about Victoria. Of course, he didn't ask for her by name, but everyone knew who he meant."

"What kind of questions?"

"Like where did we move from? How long have we been here.?" Ma shuddered. "I knew we should have gone to a lawyer and had her officially adopted."

Victoria knew as well as they that the papers would mean nothing if someone else claimed her. The thought sucked her mouth dry.

"Why did he want to know about her?"

"He wouldn't say."

Victoria hated seeing the concern in both her parents' eyes. "He left again. Guess I wasn't who he looked for."

Her parents nodded though the worry lingered in their eyes just as it did in her heart.

Pa ate his breakfast then pushed the plate aside. "I'll change into my Sunday clothes then we better get on over to the church. Who's playing today?"

"Josie." She and Eve had already gone. Stella and her children had left too.

A few minutes later Victoria followed her parents across the yard. She and Ma joined Eve in the second pew from the front where they always sat. At least here, Victoria could feel safe and sheltered.

They were about to begin when the door opened. Victoria was too well-trained to turn around until she saw the way Josie's eyes widened. On the pretext of adjusting her shawl, Victoria stole a glance. An older couple dressed like they were going to a wedding.

Or a funeral.

Obviously from the city. Why so many city visitors all of a sudden? It made Victoria twitch.

She joined the singing and listened to Pa's sermon, but she was distracted by the visitors sitting in the back.

The service ended, and she stood and turned to give

them closer study. But they hurried out the door. Victoria released a pent-up breath.

She hadn't expected Reese to come. He'd still be watching his cows. Yet, she missed him as they sat around the table for dinner. Teller and two others had joined them, though for the life of her, she couldn't remember what either of them had said their name was.

Afterwards, Stella and Blossom went to their room for a nap. Donny went outside to play with his toy barn and small farm animals.

"You girls go out and enjoy the sunshine," Ma said.

The three cowboys crowded to the door.

"Ma, do you mind if I go to my room?" Victoria had no desire to walk with the others.

"You go right ahead." Ma's gentle smile informed Victoria she understood her reluctance to go with her sisters. "I know you're missing Reese."

Upstairs, she paged through her journals. A record of her four years as a Kinsley. Would that history go on forever? She shivered. Having a strange man ask about her had upset her more than she cared to admit. *As the mountains are round about Jerusalem, so the Lord is round about his people from henceforth even for ever.* After hearing Mr. Bates talk and deciding to leave her past behind, she should not be so fearful.

But what if her past wasn't ready to leave her alone?

She lay on her bed, turning the pages of her book, *Great Painters of the World,* and remembering the time she'd shared the book with Reese. She closed the book and lay on her back. A future with a man like Reese was what she wanted. Not a man like him, but him alone.

A knock sounded downstairs. Pa answered the door.

Victoria had no desire to entertain visitors and remained where she was. She heard a man introduce himself and his wife as Mr. and Mrs. Hayworth from Chicago.

That was where Reese was from. Victoria sat up to listen.

Her parents invited them into the parlor. Their voices carried clearly up the stairs.

There was some small talk. Then Mr. Hayworth spoke. "Our daughter, Constance, disappeared four years ago. I believe the young lady you call Victoria is our daughter."

The chasm Victoria had long feared opened up and swallowed her.

As if from a great distance, she heard Pa ask for proof.

Apparently, they'd brought a picture.

Mrs. Hayworth spoke. "She has a birthmark on her left thigh. It's dark purple and V-shaped."

Darkness swirled around Victoria as she pressed her hand to a birthmark on her thigh that had that shape.

There was more conversation, but she didn't hear it. She didn't want to.

She did not want to be Constance Hayworth from Chicago.

Ma called up the stairs. "Victoria, would you please come down?"

Victoria sat up on the side of her bed. She didn't trust her legs to carry her down the stairs. *God, be my strength and comfort.*

She touched her latest journal and got to her feet. Whatever lay ahead, she would deal with it. *As the mountains are round about Jerusalem, so the Lord is round about his people from henceforth even for ever.* She said the words over and over inside her head as she went to the parlor and sank to a chair beside Ma.

Ma and Pa clutched each other's hand. For their sake, she must be strong.

She forced her attention to the couple opposite them. The man had gray hair and a thin moustache. He wore a celluloid collar and a pinstriped suit. His expression was one of strength and determination.

She looked at the woman. She'd once had blonde hair, but it had mostly faded to white. Her eyes were blue. Victoria knew she would look like that woman as she aged.

They studied her as keenly as she studied them. Mrs. Hayworth's eyes filled with tears, but she blinked them back.

Pa broke the silence. "Victoria, Mr. and Mrs. Hayworth believe you are their missing daughter."

"This is a picture of you shortly before you disappeared." Mr. Hayworth handed her the photo.

Victoria recognized herself. She felt no gladness at learning the truth. "Why have you waited so long to come?"

"We have searched far and wide," the woman said. "Every lead turned out to be nothing."

Victoria struggled to contain her anger. Why now? Just when she'd decided she could move forward?

"I've had a detective looking for you all this time," Mr. Hayworth added.

"The man who was here a few days ago. How did he finally find me?"

"I don't know if he ever would have, except a cowboy from Chicago contacted us. He remembered the publicity when you disappeared and that I had offered a sizeable reward. I'll be only too happy to give it to him now that I know it is you."

A cowboy from Chicago. Reese. No wonder he had so often suggested Victoria should welcome news about her past. Her insides cracked open and bled out. To think she had been hoping for a future with him. And all he wanted was the reward money,

"Now what?" she asked.

"We'd like to take you home," Mr. Hayworth said.

"As soon as you're ready."

Tears streamed from Victoria's eyes. Ma's too. Pa sniffed.

Home? This was home. But she'd always wondered about her past. Now was her chance to learn about it. Still, she couldn't think about leaving. "Can I have a day or two to say goodbye?"

"As long as you like, my dear." The woman seemed understanding, but the man pulled his watch from his pocket, opened and studied it, then snapped it shut.

"I can't stay long."

"She needs time, dear," the woman said in a gentle voice.

Victoria's heart felt dead. She would say her goodbyes. She would become Constance. Thanks to Reese she would leave behind all those she loved.

\* \* \*

REESE HAD SPENT a troublesome few days. He'd seen the tracks and knew a cougar stalked the cows. Every night he guarded his animals. They were restless, as if the animal was close enough for them to smell, and yet Reese never saw it.

Sunday came and went. He hoped he could ride into town before the day was over, but three cowboys rode up after dinner. They introduced themselves as being from the neighboring ranches.

"We're getting together a bunch to hunt down that animal. It's been harassing all our cows."

"I can't leave my herd. I'm here alone."

"That's all right. We'll let you know when we find the critter. You ever lay eyes on it?"

"I've seen tracks."

"Can you show us? Maybe we can trail it from here."

Reese took them to the tracks he'd seen. "These are fresh ones."

"We'll follow them." The cowboys rode away.

Reese checked his herd, hoping none had been taken while he was away for his dinner. He'd be camping right next to the herd until that cat was found.

Two days and nights he spent there until one of the cowboys returned with news that they'd shot the big cat. "Biggest one I ever saw. But so old he was practically falling apart. Guess that's why he was looking for easy pickings. We done him a favor shooting him. He was only going to suffer."

Reese rode back to his house. Had a proper cup of coffee and thought of taking time to bake some biscuits. But his heart called him to something more important, and he saddled up and rode to town.

He saw Josie in front of the church and reined in.

She scowled at him.

He could think of no reason for her to do so. Unless someone was hurt or sick. Victoria? "What's wrong?"

"How can you even ask?"

He dismounted. "Because I don't know."

"I suppose you thought we wouldn't figure it out."

He tipped his head back and forth, trying to determine if she was joshing or serious. She looked pretty serious. He glanced toward the manse, hoping Victoria would appear and help him sort this out. She didn't. "Would you please explain what's going on?"

"She's gone. I hope you're happy."

"Who?" And why should he be happy?

"Stop pretending. Victoria is gone to Chicago. Thanks to you."

He raced toward the house, knocked, and then barged in without waiting for an invite. "She's gone? When? What happened?"

Mr. and Mrs. Kinsley looked up from drinking tea. The preacher waved him to a chair.

Mr. Kinsley waited until Reese sat down before he spoke. "Mr. and Mrs. Hayworth from Chicago came and claimed her as their daughter. She's gone back with them. As she should."

Reese couldn't speak past the darkness filling his thoughts.

Mrs. Kinsley sighed softly. "You knew who she was, didn't you?"

"I suspected it the first day I saw her. I'd seen her in Chicago with her father. When she told me about her accident, I was almost certain and wrote to my mother to ask if the Hayworth girl had returned home. When she said no, I knew it was Victoria." He turned to the preacher. "I wanted to tell her, but I wanted to speak to you first so she would be surrounded by your love." He groaned. "I waited too long."

Josie had followed him. "I hope you enjoy your reward money."

He jerked around to face her. "You think I told the Hayworths in order to get money?" He shook his head. "You don't know me at all if you believe that."

"They said someone from Chicago saw her and let them know. Who else would it be?"

He told them about Smitty. Not that he'd known the man was from Chicago, but he could be from anywhere that suited his purposes. "All he cares about is the money." Not how this would upset Victoria's life.

The preacher nodded. "It's a relief to know it wasn't you. But Victoria believes it was."

Reese shoved his chair back. He strode from the room, ignoring the preacher's call to wait.

He hadn't been honest with her. He wasn't any better than Betty had been to him.

Now it was too late. She had returned to being Constance Hayworth. A rich girl living in a fine mansion in the city.

Not that he'd ever had any hope that she would fit into his simple ranch home.

* * *

"Constance, your cousins have come to welcome you home."

"Yes, Mother." Victoria had to remind herself she was Constance. She went toward the parlor. One of many rooms in this house. And like the others, it was overfull of fancy furniture and china figurines, with beautiful paintings on the walls. When left on her own, she went from one room to another, solely to admire the artwork.

The Hayworths had pieced together Victoria's disappearance to their satisfaction. She'd simply vanished one day. They considered every possibility—kidnapping, accident, lost and attacked by a wild animal. Two days after her disappearance, they had received a cryptic note. *It will cost ya to get her back.* It arrived after a search had begun, after authorities had begun their extensive search, after her father had interviewed men at the foundry.

Victoria assumed Reese had been one of those men. Had her father angered him enough that this was his way of revenge? Even though Reese was only sixteen at the time, he was a man doing a man's job, and would be under as much suspicion as any of the others.

When no further communication was received, her father and the authorities had determined the note was simply opportunistic. Someone hoping to profit from her disappearance. They hoped that their daughter was alive somewhere, perhaps held prisoner. But perhaps she was dead. They continued the search, always hopeful, yet afraid but needing to know.

But now it seemed the reason there'd been no more messages was that whoever had Victoria had been killed in the train accident. The Hayworths, the authorities, no one had known she was on that train—four days away from Chicago. They were grateful the Kinsleys had seen her in the hospital as they helped with the injured and taken her into their family when no relatives could be found for her.

A nice, neat explanation that did nothing to make Victoria's adjustment any easier.

She took two steadying breaths before she entered the parlor and was greeted by two young ladies about her age. They simpered and fluttered their hands and eyes. It was all Victoria could do not to sigh.

Smiling and nodding as she listened to these unfamiliar cousins, she wished she could still be Victoria Kinsley.

"How quaint that you were in a preacher's family," the one named Agatha said with a shudder. "So many constraints. I cannot begin to fathom what it would be like."

"I'm sure you can't." If only they knew that her life in Chicago had many more restraints than life with the Kinsleys. A few days after her arrival, she had gone to the kitchen and offered to help. The cook blanched. The maid helping the cook fluttered her apron as if to ward off a fainting spell, and Mrs. Hayworth—Mother—had rushed Victoria from the kitchen.

"Don't bother the help. It upsets them."

The other cousin, Effie, leaned forward with a sly smile. "Were the cowboys handsome?"

Victoria had enough of the conversation. She fluttered her eyelashes. "Oh yes. You can't imagine how handsome they are riding those wild horses and swinging a rope while yelling 'Yahoo' at the top of their lungs." She sighed dramatically.

Both cousins pressed their wrists to their foreheads and pretended to swoon.

They stayed another half hour that seemed ten hours

long then bid farewell. "We are having a party on Saturday in honor of your safe return."

"Thank you." She leaned her forehead against the door, wishing she didn't have to attend.

Mother Hayworth touched Victoria's shoulder, making her jump and press her hand to her chest.

"I didn't mean to startle you. I know this is hard for you, but things will get easier in time."

"I suppose so."

"Come, let's sit and do needlework. You used to like that."

She'd begun to work on a needlepoint piece that would cover a footstool. She picked it up to add stitches but after a few minutes she put it aside. "May I play the piano?"

"By all means."

She played several pieces, but one kept calling to her. The hymn Reese had sung with them. She closed her eyes and played it, her heart pouring forth sorrow and regret.

Mother Hayworth touched her shoulder. "You're crying." She handed Victoria a monogramed handkerchief.

"I'm sorry," Victoria mumbled as she wiped her eyes.

"Come, let's go for a walk."

She obediently went outside. Mother pulled Victoria's arm through hers as they followed the pathways through the groomed gardens.

"You were such a sweet baby. Always smiling and laughing. Everyone commented on what a good-natured child you were. How your father loved to take you for drives in the buggy."

Victoria listened, trying to associate who she was with who this woman talked about.

They returned to the house. "It will get easier," Mother Hayworth said.

"I know. May I go to my room?"

"Certainly."

Victoria kept her pace sedate as she climbed the wide, sweeping staircase and went down the hall, passing so many empty rooms to the one she'd been given. Here were items of her past. A fancy china doll. A collection of books. Schoolbooks that Victoria had looked at, wishing she could take them to Glory and use them to teach the children there.

She opened her last journal. She had not written in it since she'd left Glory. Hadn't even opened it, but did so now, wanting to touch that life she'd known.

Words were written below her last entry.

*We'll miss you but hope you have a good life. Eve.*

*I'll be all alone in our big bed. Josie.*

*I'd give up my horse to see you back. Flora.*

*It don't seem right that you are going. Stella.*

*I will always think of you with love. You own a piece of my heart. Ma.*

*May God be with you, my child. Pa*

*I want to hear more about the French. Jimmy.* Those words were crudely printed. Victoria guessed someone had helped him with the spelling. Who would teach the children now?

*I wish we could be part of who you are now. Lisa.*

*You and Reese belong together. Sylvie.*

Victoria closed the book. She had trusted Reese. He didn't deserve it.

She sat on the floor, several journals spread out before her. She told herself she wouldn't read the entries about Reese but she couldn't resist, and pulled the latest journal to her lap.

She read about her first walk with him, her longing to know who she was, her fear that she would find out and lose the world she knew. She read how he'd made her laugh. The days she'd gone by the livery barn to visit with him. How often she had watched him up on the ladder painting...something he didn't know. She pored over the passages when she recorded Reese telling her that to know her past was better than to always worry about it. Mr. Bates had made her see she must let the past go.

Over and over, she read the words, trying to sort out her life.

If Reese had informed the Hayworths about her, was it for the reward money or because he wanted her to be free of her fear of her past?

But was she free of it, or trapped by it?

Was informing the Hayworths a self-serving act on Reese's behalf or a loving one for her sake? Either way, could she forgive him for the disruption it had caused?

Her legs began to tingle, and she realized she'd been sitting on the floor a long time. She rose, waited for the pins and needles to go away, then went downstairs.

Her father had returned. "Join us for tea." Mother Hayworth sat nearby.

She waited until the tea was served by a maid then asked permission to speak.

"Certainly," her father said.

"How much money did you give Reese Cartwright for

letting you know where I was?" She didn't know why it mattered. Perhaps so she could measure her worth against the amount.

"It was a thousand dollars."

She gasped. "So much." No wonder Reese wanted it.

"But I didn't give it to a Cartwright. The man's name who claimed the reward was Smitty."

"Smitty." She barely managed to set her cup and saucer down without dropping it.

"I assume you know the man?"

"Barely. He wasn't the sort I would associate with."

"It's a relief to hear that."

She jerked to her feet and paced the room. She'd misjudged Reese. She should have known he wouldn't do anything to hurt her.

She went from one window to another.

"Constance, please sit down."

Victoria stared out at the rose garden. She was allowed to smell them but not pull out a weed or pluck a dead leaf, and if she wanted a bouquet, she must ask the gardener to cut one for her.

"Constance, please." Then, "Victoria."

Victoria startled at the sound of her name.

"Please sit down. You're making me dizzy." Her mother kept her voice gentle, but Victoria thought she caught a nervous tone.

She sat. Or rather, she perched on the edge of her chair. *Lord, help me say what I need to say.*

"I know you are my parents, and I was your daughter for fourteen years. But I don't remember it. This is all strange to me. I don't fit in. I have dreams and goals that don't belong here. I want to teach." She wanted to marry and be a rancher's wife. She couldn't do both. It seemed her life was full of hard choices. "I'm asking you, begging you, to let me return to Glory."

Father's face darkened. Mother's blanched.

"Please," Victoria whispered.

Father shook his head, but before he could speak, Mother did. "Please leave us alone to discuss this."

She gladly hurried from the room and upstairs. She gathered her journals together. *Oh, Reese, forgive me for misjudging you.*

It was all she could do not to pack up her things.

As she waited, she prayed that she might be able to return to the life she knew, that Reese would accept her and forgive her. Her heart thrilled at the idea of becoming a rancher's wife.

If he didn't ask her, she could always go back to her original plan of teaching.

A maid came to the door. "Your parents would like you to go to the parlor."

Her heart beating too rapidly, Victoria followed the maid downstairs, stepped into the room, and sat on the chair her father indicated. She grew dizzy as she looked from one to the other. They did not look pleased.

Her mother broke the tension. "We had hoped bringing you home would enable you to remember. It's been two weeks, and you remember nothing. The doctor says you won't. We realize you are not happy here."

Victoria nodded agreement to all this.

Her father held up a hand to signal he would speak. "I bow to your mother's opinion that we should let you return to the life you know."

Victoria's breath whooshed out.

"We have a few conditions though."

Victoria would agree to most anything at this point.

"We'd like to be involved in your life."

She waited, wondering what that meant.

Mother noticed her tension. "We'd like to be able to visit you from time to time and ask that you visit us on occasion as well."

"Of course. When can I go home?"

"We'll make arrangements to take you back as soon as possible."

Father sighed. "We'll plan to leave in two days."

"Thank you." She hugged them both and raced upstairs. Two day plus travel time. She would be home soon.

\* \* \*

REESE RODE THUNDER at a pace that caused the horse to break into a sweat. It had been more than two weeks since Victoria had left for Chicago. Two weeks of agony as he tried to think what to do. He could write a letter and explain he wasn't the one to tell the Hayworths. Though it didn't really make a difference.

He had known but not told her. He was no better than Betty, and the knowledge burned at his insides. Truth and trust were two things he valued, but he had not given them to Victoria. Even if he wrote her or, better yet, traveled to Chicago and spoke to her in person, how could he ever expect her to trust him?

Day after day, he rode hard. He worked hard also, sweating equally as hard as poor Thunder did. On

Sunday, he went to church but refused an invitation to join the Kinsleys for a meal.

Each of them had assured him that they forgave him for not telling them the truth and didn't blame him for what happened.

If only he could forgive himself.

He reined in on a knoll and walked Thunder to cool him. Then he sat on the grass and looked at the land before him.

Land that he had once thought the prettiest he'd ever seen now seemed colorless and flat.

As he sat there, he made up his mind. He would go to Chicago and beg her forgiveness. He would get a job in the foundry again so he could be close to her whether she welcomed his friendship or not.

Having made up his mind, he swung into the saddle and returned home. He started to pack then realized he'd have to make arrangements for the land and cattle before he left. He'd simply go to the neighbor to the north and turn it all over to him. Sell at a loss. It didn't matter. He just wanted to get to Chicago.

He rode to the neighbors that afternoon. There was no one home. The cattle would be all right for a few days. At some point, he would have to make arrangements for them but not today.

He could not return to his mockingly empty house. No, he'd go to town, let the Kinsleys know of his plans, and arrange a train ticket.

Having already given Thunder a hard workout, he kept to a steady canter as he rode to town.

* * *

MA AND PA welcomed Victoria and the Hayworths with open arms. Victoria wept in her Ma's embrace. "I've come home," she whispered.

Ma and Pa waited for an explanation.

"She's pining for the home she knows," Mother Hayworth said. "I couldn't stand by and watch her suffer." She explained their conditions, and everyone eagerly agreed.

"You've taken good care of our child," Father Hayworth said. "Is there anything I can do to repay you?"

"Bringing her back is the best thing you could do."

"Wait," Victoria said. "There is something you can do."

The four parents looked surprised.

"Father, you know that detective you hired? Well, he's going to need another job. Why don't you ask him to look for the Kinsley's son, Josh?"

"Done."

Pa and Father shook hands.

The Hayworths did not want to linger, but agreed to stay in town a few days, taking a room at the hotel.

As soon as they left, Victoria hugged her sisters and parents. She couldn't stop laughing and crying.

"Victoria," Pa said. "There is something you should know. It wasn't Reese who wanted the reward."

"I know. It was Smitty. I should have never doubted Reese. He may never forgive me."

Josie and Eve looked at each other and chuckled.

"What?" Victoria demanded.

"Reese has been acting like a bear with a thorn in his paw."

She narrowed her eyes at her sisters. "Is that supposed to be good news?"

"It's because you're not here."

"How do you know that? He tell you?"

Josie shrugged. "I've got eyes." She and Eve laughed again.

Victoria ignored them. She wouldn't rest until she'd seen Reese and apologized. "I know I just got home but I'd like a ride out to see Reese. Pa, would you take me?"

"Child, right now, if you asked me to take you to the ocean, I would agree."

Josie and Eve whispered together, "Ask him, ask him. We'd like to see the ocean."

She pretended to swat them away.

"I'll go get a wagon." Pa left. He returned so quickly she knew he didn't have time to get to the livery barn and back.

"Did you change your mind?"

"Yup." He guided Victoria to the window and pointed toward the river.

Reese stood on the path.

"He's waiting for you."

Victoria was out the door before Pa finished. She hurried across the yard and stopped in front of Reese.

"You're back," he said

"You're here," she said.

"I have things to say to you."

"I have things to say to you," she echoed.

"Let's get away from all those people peering out the window."

She laughed. "It's good to be home."

They walked side by side toward the river, through the trees and to the grassy slope.

"Shall we sit?" he asked.

She sat, relieved when he sat close enough to brush her arm with his.

"I hope you can forgive me," he said at exactly the same moment as she said the same words. They both laughed.

"Ladies first."

"Reese, I doubted you. I judged you. I thought you'd contacted the Hayworths for the reward money." She held up her hand when he tried to interrupt. "Let me finish. To my credit, I had already wondered if I was wrong before Father Hayworth told me it was Smitty. I'm asking for your forgiveness."

"I readily forgive you, but you might change your mind when you hear what I have to say. You see, I thought you were Constance Hayworth the minute I saw you. To be certain, I wrote my mother and she said you were still missing. I planned to tell you, but I wanted your ma and pa to be there when I did. When your pa had to be away, I delayed. But I could have told you anytime. I'm sorry I didn't. I kept the truth from you, and that was wrong."

"I realize you did it because you wanted to protect me."

"Does that mean you forgive me?"

"It does."

"And now you're back to teach."

She tried to think how to inform him she was open to other alternatives without appearing too bold. But she couldn't think of a way. Besides, she was tired of secrets and mistakes. She would make sure he understood clearly what she meant.

"I will teach if I have no other option, but my dream for my future has changed."

"It has?" He sounded like he'd swallowed a frog. "What do you want now?"

She shifted so she looked into his dark eyes. Oh, how she'd missed those, and that bronze face now wearing those little worry lines by his lips. She touched those lines. "I want it all. I want a little ranch house with three bedrooms, a garden spot, perhaps a cat and a dog." She paused, letting him digest that.

"I want to look out the door and see a dark-haired cowboy on a black horse, riding home. I want to look out the kitchen window and see a favorite picnic spot." She nodded. "I want it all."

He caught her hands and brought them to his chest. "I want the same things. Well, not the cowboy, but someone waiting for me at home. Someone I trust wholly and who trusts me completely because the truth has set us free." He leaned closer. "Victoria, I want that person to be you."

She leaned closer for his kiss.

He pulled back. "I'm not a rich man."

"If that mattered to me, I would have stayed in Chicago."

"I was in the process of making plans to go there. I thought I'd get a job at the foundry."

"Why would you do that? You don't like the city and hated working in the foundry."

"It was the only way I could think that would let me see you."

"You would do that for me? Why?"

"Because I love you."

She laughed. "Good, because I love you."

"Will you marry me?"

"Yes, a thousand times yes."

He caught her lips in a tender, sweet, lingering kiss that promised a future full of everything she could ever wish for.

## CHAPTER 13

Josie and Eve squealed when they heard the news.

Ma and Pa were hesitant until Victoria explained, "I have spent too much of my life afraid of the future. But now I'm not."

"We only want you to be happy." Ma hugged her.

"The Hayworths are still in town," Pa said. "You need to speak to them."

"Of course." She and Reese stepped out of the house.

Reese held back. "I worked for your father. He was pretty hard to take." He told her how her father had practically accused all the men at the foundry of having something to do with his daughter's disappearance.

"He probably doesn't even remember it."

"I suppose not." They met the Hayworths in the hotel lobby.

"This is the man I am going to marry," Victoria said after introductions had been made. As she'd said, her father didn't even remember Reese.

"But we know nothing about him," her mother protested.

"You are both invited out to my ranch tomorrow. I'll show you the place where we will live."

Father agreed.

* * *

THEY PLANNED to leave right after breakfast. Reese had arranged for Sylvie to prepare a proper meal. He retrieved it from her before he picked up the Hayworths at the hotel.

Sylvie had already discovered the visitors and knew who they were. "Glad they brought Victoria home."

"We're going to get married," Reese said, and had the satisfaction of giving her news she didn't already have.

"Well, that don't surprise me none. But I'm warning you, you treat that girl like gold, or you'll answer to me."

"Yes, ma'am." He saluted and chuckled to think how Victoria would laugh when he told her about Sylvie.

He picked up the Hayworths and Victoria and they traveled to the ranch. Knowing Mr. Hayworth's reputation as a savvy businessman, Reese carefully pointed out the richness of the grass, the promise of the burgeoning cattle industry, and how Montana was growing.

He gave them a tour of the house then took Mr. Hayworth to see his cows, leaving Victoria to entertain her mother. They arrived back at the house in time for the dinner Sylvie had prepared, and then they returned to town.

It wasn't until they were almost back that Mr. Hayworth gave his opinion. He spoke to Victoria. "Your young man seems to know his business. I expect he will do well." It was high praise from the man.

The Hayworths agreed that a wedding before they returned to Chicago was rushed, but they wanted to be there, so it would have to be so.

* * *

Mother Hayworth wanted to send to Chicago for a proper wedding gown.

Ma wanted to make one for Victoria.

Victoria reminded them both that there wasn't time. "A simple gown will have to do."

Miss Sylvie trundled over to the parsonage and said Victoria must go back to the diner with her. Wondering what the woman wanted, Victoria did so.

Sylvie led her into her bedroom and opened a trunk. She lifted out a frothy wedding dress. "You will wear this."

Victoria fingered the skirt. "It beautiful, but where did you get it?" And why? It seemed so out of character for the big, brash woman.

"I was once married. Many years ago. He died, and here I am." She giggled. "I'll let you in on a little secret. I might be getting married again."

"How exciting. Who is the lucky man?"

"Don't pretend you don't know. It's Earl Douglas."

"Don't you want to save this dress for that occasion?"

Sylvie laughed so hard tears streamed down her face. When she sobered, she held the dress up to her wide body. "How do you think I'd squeeze myself into this?"

"Umm. It might be difficult."

"Pshaw. It would be impossible. You take it home and press it and wear it for your wedding. When is the big day?"

"Saturday."

"Girl, that's day after tomorrow. How do you plan to get ready by then?"

"We'll be ready. All it takes is standing up before my pa and promising now and forever."

Sylvie's eyes grew dreamy. "It's that simple, isn't it?"

Two days later Victoria donned her borrowed finery and admired the floating layers of silk.

"It's beautiful," Ma said.

"I'd have to agree," Mother added.

Victoria's sisters had already left and waited for them in the vestibule.

Pa had left and also waited at the church.

Her Hayworth parents and her ma escorted her across the yard to the church. She peeked into the sanctuary and gasped at the crowd. "I didn't expect anyone to come."

"Everyone is happy for you."

Kade led Victoria's two mothers down the aisle and seated them.

Flora began to play the Bridal Chorus.

Victoria took her Hayworth father's arm and stepped into the aisle.

Reese was handsome in a black suit and white shirt. His dark eyes held her gaze as she walked toward him.

They repeated their vows before Pa and the gathered audience. They signed the official papers then Pa introduced them.

# A LOVE TO CHERISH

"May I present Mr. and Mrs. Reese Cartwright. May the Lord bless your union."

Amidst clapping they hurried down the aisle.

Victoria shouldn't have been surprised that the women of the area had put together a nice lunch. But she didn't taste a bit of it. Couldn't remember if she even ate.

Finally, someone brought a wagon to the church and Reese lifted her into it.

As they headed home, Reese said, "When your pa had us say, 'I plight thee my troth' I made my own vow." He stopped the wagon and took her hands in his. "Victoria, I pledge thee truth and trust forever."

Her heart so full there was hardly room for her words, she said, "Reese, I pledge thee my past, my present, and my future. Every minute of my life from now until the Lord calls me home. I hope to always make you happy."

"You have filled my heart to overflowing." He kissed her soundly. Then they drove on toward home and a shared life.

## ALSO BY LINDA FORD

**Buffalo Gals of Bonners Ferry series**

Glory and the Rawhide Preacher

Mandy and the Missouri Man

Joanna and the Footloose Cowboy

**Circle A Cowboys series**

Dillon

Mike

Noah

Adam

Sam

Pete

Austin

**Romancing the West**

Jake's Honor

Cash's Promise

Blaze's Hope

Levi's Blessing

A Heart's Yearning

A Heart's Blessing

A Heart's Delight

A Heart's Promise

**Glory, Montana - the Preacher's Daughters**

Loving a Rebel

A Love to Cherish

Renewing Love

A Love to Have and Hold

**Glory, Montana - The Cowboys**

Cowboy Father

Cowboy Groom

Cowboy Preacher

**Glory, Montana - Frontier Brides**

Rancher's Bride

Hunter's Bride

Christmas Bride

**Wagon Train Romance series**

Wagon Train Baby

Wagon Train Wedding

Wagon Train Matchmaker

Wagon Train Christmas

Renewed Love

Rescued Love

Reluctant Love

Redeemed Love

**Dakota Brides series**

Temporary Bride

Abandoned Bride

Second-Chance Bride

Reluctant Bride

**Prairie Brides series**

Lizzie

Maryelle

Irene

Grace

**Wild Rose Country**

Crane's Bride

Hannah's Dream

Chastity's Angel

Cowboy Bodyguard

Copyright © 2018 by Linda Ford

All rights reserved.

No part of this book may be reproduced in any form or by any electronic or mechanical means, including information storage and retrieval systems, without written permission from the author, except for the use of brief quotations in a book review.

Printed in Great Britain
by Amazon